INFINITY'S EDGE

KEN LOZITO

ACOUSTICAL BOOKS LLC

Published by Acoustical Books, LLC

KenLozito.com

Cover design by Jeff Brown

Editor: Myra Shelley

Proofreader: Tamara Blain

IF YOU WOULD LIKE TO BE NOTIFIED WHEN MY NEXT BOOK IS RELEASED VISIT - WWW.KENLOZITO.COM

ISBN: 978-1-945223-08-2

CHAPTER ONE

Thirty years ago, Edward Johnson had been an outstanding young intelligence officer working for the Department of Homeland Security when he'd caught the attention of billionaire Bruce Matherson, Chief Executive Officer of Dux Corporation. For about a year, Bruce had repeatedly tried to recruit Ed before Ed decided to see what a company like Dux Corporation—known for its various military contracts and weapons development technology—was all about. He'd had no idea what was in store for him or how important a man the late great Bruce Matherson really had been.

Plenty of billionaires believed they were visionaries of the future, but it just so happened that Bruce Matherson actually was and had been tasked with the preservation of the Human race. Early on, Bruce had taken Ed into his confidence. He'd been shown the first-contact videos that were withheld from Project Stargate during the nineteen-eighties. Later, in the year twenty-fifteen, the New Horizons spacecraft had flown by Pluto and taken the first ever high-resolution photographs of the dwarf planet's surface, showing what they now knew as a Boxan outpost, and confirming what scientists had long suspected: they weren't alone in the galaxy.

Proof that intelligent life did exist in the galaxy had been kept from the general public. The fact that these intelligent life-forms knew of Human existence and were watching had also been withheld, and Ed couldn't imagine what it must have been like for Bruce.

Ed had joined Dux Corp a few years after the New Horizons' discovery, and it was another ten years before Bruce brought Ed into the inner circle, which was responsible for funding scientific research across the globe. Bruce had always suspected that the Russian equivalent of Project Stargate had received the same mysterious Boxan message through a psychic link that hadn't been fully understood, but there was no way they could have known about the Boxan outpost on Pluto until recently. The current world stage was vastly different from what it had been in the nineteen-eighties with China's rise as a global superpower. Somehow, it had become Ed's job to get all these nations to work together as humanity stepped to the brink of taking an evolutionary leap into the wider cosmos. Truth be told, Ed would have preferred at least another hundred years to develop the technology they needed to go out into the galaxy and face the challenges they were about to face.

Ed sat in the war room at the North American Aerospace Defense Command, or as it was better known, NORAD, and glanced around the large oval conference table where a holodisplay was beaming the solar system ten feet above its surface. Various military officials and directors from the different intelligence agencies sat, engaging in small talk as they waited. Lining the walls were banks of blank holoscreens that would remain so until the meeting began.

A firm hand touched Ed's shoulder, and he looked up at Iris Barrett. On digital paper, she was his assistant who handled his schedule, which she did quite effectively, but truthfully she was his protector. Iris had state-of-the-art neural implants and reinforced muscle tissue made possible with nanite technology, and her blood had been engineered for quick healing beyond even the capabilities of the military.

"Five minutes, sir," Iris said. She wore a black business suit, and her short black hair was pulled back into a tight bun.

Ed nodded.

Bruce Matherson's original plan had been for the 'discovery' of the Boxan outpost on Pluto to be 'rediscovered' in another ten years, but Zack Quick had put an end to all of that after he'd released the original New Horizons images to the general public. Zack's actions had been the catalyst that changed the destination of the Athena mission, which had originally been Titan. The mission to Titan was to have been Kaylan Farrow's test run for a later mission to Pluto, but she'd ended up on an urgent mission to Pluto first, and then the Athena had disappeared into space.

They'd finally received a mission update from the Athena, and it raised more questions and concerns than it answered. Ed had watched the video logs over a hundred times in an attempt to glean all the information available, but he had to admit that if they'd stuck to Bruce's original plan, an additional ten years might have been too late for the people of Earth. It was an interesting thought that had become more prevalent in his mind and the minds of the younger generation around him.

Old world national borders had increasingly become blurred in their more advanced society. While they were far from united as a species, Ed had noticed the increasing change in perspective regarding national identity of late; however, he wasn't foolish enough to believe that the world would unite to meet this alien threat. No, those perceptions were mere seedlings of a plant that had yet to bear any fruit, and if they had another hundred years, they might be much better prepared. Besides, a hundred years from now the problems they were currently facing would have decidedly fallen into someone else's lap, which Ed would have preferred when exhaustion seemed to be crushing him. He felt his lips curve upward in a half smile at the thought. He knew he would do his utmost both for his late friend and for the people of Earth.

Colonel John Hines called for the meeting to start. The large, dark-skinned man stood ramrod straight, and his chiseled features gave him the appearance of the Greek Titan Atlas personified.

Edward Johnson stood up, and those in the military snapped a salute as four-star general William Sheridan entered the war room. Ed still had to resist the urge to raise his hand and snap a salute with the rest of them, but his military days were long gone, more than half a lifetime ago.

General Sheridan swung his mighty gaze around the room and acknowledged them all with a single, no-nonsense nod.

"Sir, the president is connecting," Colonel Hines said.

They sat down, and Ed tried to recall what he knew about General Sheridan. He came from a long line of enlisted men and women. He'd made a name for himself in the fight against global terrorist organizations and had risen through the ranks during his thirty-five-year career. If there ever was another world war, General Sheridan stood a good chance at getting that fifth star and ascending to Commander of Armies for the United States. Ed could think of worse choices for the president to have put on point for this.

The holoscreens blinked to life as President Susan Halloway came to prominence. The other holoscreens were occupied by the vice president and joint chiefs.

"Madam President, thank you for coming," Sheridan greeted.

"General Sheridan," the president said. She glanced at those in the room, and Ed would have sworn that her gaze lingered on him for a moment.

The general nodded to Colonel Hines. Hines's thick neck muscles rolled as he swung his gaze to the far end of the table. "Dr. Gray, you have the floor."

Dr. Philip Gray, Scientific Advisor to the President, stood up. Ed suppressed a groan and couldn't for the life of him figure out why Halloway kept Gray on as a scientific advisor. Family connections at their finest.

"We're here to discuss the recent Athena mission update that we received two weeks ago. We've circulated some of the details through the FBI, along with a complete update to the CIA and NSA. Their findings confirm that the testimonies provided by the Athena crew, while compelling, should not be accepted at face value," Dr. Gray said.

"Which part?" General Sheridan asked.

"There were multiple inconsistencies in their reports, with no fewer than two of their crewmembers under the direct compulsion of the alien species identified as the Xiiginn," Dr. Gray said.

"Only Jonah Redford is showing outward signs of being

under Xiiginn compulsion," Ed said, drawing an annoyed look from Gray. "Zack was cleared by Dr. Goodwin."

"Yes, we have her report as well, but she also indicated it's possible that Mr. Quick's symptoms simply hadn't manifested yet."

Ed shook his head, brows raised. "He was held captive by the Xiiginn. Even the Boxans don't understand why he's immune." Ed turned his gaze to the president. "Brenda Goodwin is an excellent medical doctor, as well as a psychiatrist. We should trust her opinion. Brenda is just acknowledging the possibility that Zack is under Xiiginn compulsion, but she doesn't have any evidence whatsoever to support it. She'd be remiss in her duties if she didn't at least highlight the possibility."

Halloway looked at the general questioningly.

General Sheridan cleared his throat. "In my experience, anyone held prisoner, even under extraordinary circumstances such as this, will show signs of PTSD. Goodwin's analysis of Mr. Quick appears sound. Given what the crew of the Athena has had to deal with, I think we can all acknowledge that they are under a lot of stress, which would appear in any intelligence report."

There were several chuckles from around the room.

"Madam President," Sheridan said, and all the people in the room immediately hushed, "I'm more concerned with the assertion that these aliens will come to our solar system. Regardless of whether it's these Boxans or Xiiginns, both have the potential for catastrophic effects on the Human race."

Halloway nodded. "I appreciate your opinion. Ed Johnson, what do you think?"

All eyes in the room focused on Ed, and his pulse quickened.

"The Xiiginns are the enemy. They are the real threat, and we need to prepare for them. The Boxans might become our allies."

"You would lay the fate of the Human race on 'might'?" Sheridan asked.

"They're already helping the crew of the Athena," Ed replied.

"Are you familiar with safe harbor?" Sheridan asked, and Ed shook his head. "Sea captains are under obligation to give aid to any vessel in need and provide safe passage to the nearest port. What this Boxan, Kladomaor, is doing is that." Sheridan looked up at the holoscreen of the president. "Based on all the evidence, these two alien species have been fighting a war for some time, and how many other species have been caught in the crossfire? We're at a severe disadvantage if they come here."

"What are you suggesting?" Halloway asked.

"That we prepare for imminent invasion. Start leveraging our resources, both at home and beyond, to give us some protection for the Ark Program," Sheridan said.

Ed's gut clenched. "This isn't a time to wall ourselves away in a mountain, hoping to ride out a storm."

General Sheridan's brows pushed forward severely. "The fact that you're even aware of the Ark Program is enough for me to have you taken into custody by the FBI."

Ed turned toward the president and swallowed hard. "Madam President, the world has changed so fast, and we're stumbling to catch up. I have the highest respect for General Sheridan, and his recommendation is in line with what an officer in the United States military *should* recommend. But the fact is that we can't stand against the threat of the Xiiginn on our own. We *have* to reach out to the other nations and form a coalition of forces whose sole purpose is to defend the Earth from an alien invasion. No nation on this planet can stand alone against this threat."

President Halloway's dark-eyed gaze regarded Ed for a few moments, and then she looked away. "Go ahead, Philip."

Dr. Gray cleared his throat, and Ed looked over at him. "Both alien species are keenly interested in what the Boxans refer to as the Mardoxian trait. Dux Corp, or one of its subsidiaries, developed the psychic warrior initiative in secret. Since these aliens are so interested in this ability, the general intelligence community needs to understand it better."

Ed frowned. So this was what they were after. "What are you asking, Philip?"

Philip Gray narrowed his gaze. "That you immediately turn over all research and findings of the psychic warrior initiative to the United States government as a matter of national security."

Ed chewed on the inside of his bottom lip for a moment. "What you're demanding of me and Dux Corp is entirely illegal."

"This is non-negotiable," Philip said.

Ed looked over at the president. "I know you can freeze our assets and try and take what we've built, but it will do you no good. I'm willing to give you what you ask for in return for something else."

Ed heard the shuffling footsteps of the military police heading toward him. Iris Barrett stiffened behind him but otherwise remained motionless.

"You don't make demands of the president—" Philip Gray started to say, but Halloway interrupted.

"What is it that you want?" she asked.

Ed met the president's gaze. "I want you to reach out to China, Russia, the European Union, and the rest of the United

Nations with a proposal that a coalition force be formed to deal with the alien threat. At this moment, a formal proposal of the Earth Coalition Force is being sent to your office. I ask that you and your staff review it and open communications with all the nations of this world. This is a burden that should be shared by all. Do this, and I guarantee you will have unfettered access to all of Dux Corp's research on everything since its inception."

There was a collective breath held in the war room. There weren't many who would make a demand or veiled ultimatum to the leader of the free world. Ed knew that if he were taken into custody, another of the inner circle would take over and help the people of Earth fight as best they could, although in his heart of hearts he didn't believe it would be enough. Not now. They needed the governments of the world to set aside their differences and work together.

"General Sheridan," Halloway said.

Ed felt the MPs closing in on him, but his chips were on the table and he'd bet everything on this moment.

"Yes, Madam President."

"I want you and my chief of staff to appoint a committee to formally review this Earth Coalition Force proposal that Ed has so boldly sent us. I want to know your thoughts and opinions on it before we even consider sharing it with other world leaders," President Halloway said.

"I'm at your disposal, Madam President."

Ed swallowed. The fact that they were even considering it was a good sign, but it was still a long road ahead. He glanced at Iris and nodded.

"Thank you, Madam President," Ed said. "As a show of good

faith, my assistant is sending the first of seven encrypted data caches to your office."

"First of seven!" Philip exclaimed. "You should be sending everything."

Ed leveled his gaze at him. "That's why you're only an advisor, Philip, and not the president."

Philip's face contorted to several shades of red, but he remained silent.

Ed had made some enemies, but hopefully his actions would be looked upon by future generations as having benefitted humanity, as long as there were any of them left to do the looking.

CHAPTER TWO

D ale Hicks sat in the Athena's mess hall, polishing off his breakfast with a cup of black coffee. He'd never been one for cream or sugar, preferring the bitter taste and heady aroma of freshly ground coffee. He glanced at the coffee maker. If he lived to see Michael Hunsicker again, he would thank him for insisting on bringing this glorious piece of equipment that made what NASA had anticipated as a long journey to Titan more bearable.

The Athena's original mission had been to one of Saturn's moons, but thanks to the actions of one Zack Quick, that mission had to be put on hold so they could go to Pluto instead. It had been either fate or luck that had put Pluto's orbit relatively near Earth during that fateful mission—at least that's what he and Katie Garcia had been told when Edward Johnson recruited them for the Athena's mission. Though only months had passed since they'd journeyed and gotten boots down on Pluto—an achievement worthy of the history books

—they were light years from home, chasing a Boxan legend about an alien race called the Drars, who'd fought an intergalactic war that had wiped them out. When they'd first escaped the Boxan space station destroyed by the Xiiginns, Hicks had believed they were only a few days away from figuring out what had happened to the Drars, but almost two months later they were still chasing a mysterious signal that Zack had stumbled onto right before they'd escaped. Signal wasn't even the right word. Zack had tried to explain it to him, and they'd essentially been following a trail of cosmic bread-crumbs left by a race of beings that predated Humans by tens of thousands of years.

Hicks cocked his head to the side and cracked his neck. It was a bad habit, but it just felt so good that he couldn't stop himself. An alarm showed on his internal heads-up display, but he killed it instantly, finishing his coffee. The hardened ceramic composite that comprised the Athena's outer hull had been designed for Earth's solar system, not traipsing along in interstellar space. Even with Kladomaor's help, he was beginning to think the crew of the Athena was living in a ticking timebomb.

"Hicks," Kaylan's voice said over his PDA.

"Good morning, Commander. I saw the alarm. It's on the section Vitomir and I are going to check on our EVA this morning," Hicks said.

It was alarming to think that keeping the Athena space-worthy required daily EVAs, during which they were required to patch the outer hull of the ship. How long before patching wasn't enough? Or they ran out of materials for repairs?

"Acknowledged. Please be careful," Kaylan said.

Hicks made his way down the corridor to the rear airlock.

Katie Garcia came out of one of the adjacent corridors and smiled in greeting.

"Where you off to?" Hicks asked.

"My rotation with Efren at the reactor," Katie said. Her dark hair was tied back into a ponytail.

"I thought that was on Wednesday," Hicks said.

Katie shook her head. "It is Wednesday, Major. Are you sure you're feeling okay?" she asked in a slightly amused tone.

Hicks sighed. "I'm fine. Just mixed up the days is all. How do you think the rest of them are doing?" he asked.

Katie shrugged. "They all deal with it in their own way. There's really no precedent for what we're doing."

Hicks nodded. "I'm not really sure we *should* be doing what we're doing."

Katie frowned. "What do you mean?"

"I'm not sure how much more the ship can take," Hicks said.

"Have you spoken to Kaylan about it?"

"No, not yet. I agree with the reasons for coming, but it doesn't feel like we're making any progress, and it's making me wonder why we don't head back to Earth right now."

"You should tell her."

"I will, but first we've got to keep our girl in the air," Hicks said, glancing up at the nearest monitor.

"Your concern for my well-being is noted, Major," the Athena's AI voice said through the monitor's speakers.

"I'll leave you to it, sir," Katie said and went on her way.

Hicks continued on and met Russian cosmonaut Vitomir Mikhailovich, former Commander of Titus Space Station. The bald cosmonaut was slipping into his EVA suit while being watched by Nikolai Vratowski. Trust was in short supply where

Vitomir was concerned. The former commander had attempted to sabotage the space station in an effort to join the Athena mission. The botched sabotage had claimed the lives of four people, including Vitomir's wife. Under different circumstances, Hicks would have locked Vitomir in a cell and thrown away the key, but, as the Athena's AI pointed out, not using an able-bodied person would put them outside peak efficiency—fancy words for telling them to use all available resources in order to survive.

"Major," Nikolai said. "I've included extra repair kits for this EVA, and the updated targets will appear on your HUD once you're outside."

"Thank you," Hicks said.

"I could join you if you want," Nikolai offered.

"Two at a time. That's what the commander ordered," Hicks said.

Nikolai bobbed his head and waited for the two-man team to finish donning their EVA suits.

Vitomir finished first and stood up. "Ready when you are, Major," he said.

Hicks quickly put on his suit, and Nikolai cleared them for their EVA. They stepped into the airlock and waited for the atmosphere to be sucked from the room. When the indicator lights around the door changed to green, Hicks popped the door, and there was a slight snap-hiss as the little bit of air that remained in the airlock escaped into the void.

Directly across from them was the Boxan stealth ship they'd been tagging along with since they'd left the Nershal star system. It was an impressive sight, but according to the Boxans, it was among the smaller scout-class vessels. If so, Hicks couldn't imagine what some of their bigger ships looked like. During their recent adventures, he'd gotten a glimpse of Xiiginn warships, which were sleek, wedge-shaped crafts. But Hicks knew that should anything happen to the Boxans' ship, the crew of the Athena would most likely die because their ship didn't have a Cherubian drive capable of folding space, which was the only way for them to get back to their own solar system.

"Major, we must be going," Vitomir said.

Hicks turned away and lowered the intensity of his mag boots. Tethers had already auto-locked onto the backs of their suits. Reducing the power of the mag boots enabled them to take longer strides down the Athena's hull and cover longer distances in a shorter amount of time. Beyond them was a sky full of stars the likes of which had never been seen by any Human. Gaarokk, a Boxan scientist, had pointed out that they were even beyond where the Boxans had been, since exploration had ground to a halt during their war with the Xiiginns.

"We're coming to the first series of micro-cracks," Vitomir said.

Hicks slowed down, and the two of them came to a halt. The Athena's gleaming white hull had been peppered by the small asteroid fragments they'd encountered on their long journey, creating tiny cracks.

"This grouping is bigger than the last one. I'm surprised the sensors didn't alert us sooner," Hicks said.

Being on an EVA with Vitomir was almost peaceful. Whenever Zack came along, he had this pressing need to fill the time with conversation. At least he used to. Since he'd been held prisoner by the Xiiginn, the former hacker had been much more serious. Hicks had never been a prisoner of war, but his military training had accounted for the possibility. Recovery from an ordeal like that would take time. He didn't think being aboard a spaceship was the most peaceful environment for someone suffering from PTSD, so he and Kaylan had agreed to manage Zack's stress levels, which meant cutting back on EVAs.

He and Vitomir used two repair kits to patch the fractures on the Athena's hull.

Hicks frowned and turned to Vitomir. "If Titus Station had been showing this much wear and tear, what would you have done?" he asked.

Bringing up Titus Station was never easy for Vitomir, but Hicks had to leverage the former commander's expertise. Regardless of what he'd done, he'd been responsible for Titus Station's upkeep for close to two years.

"Our fabricators were located in the subterranean levels of the asteroid we were on, and we could eventually replace entire sections of the station if we needed to. So the situation is different here. There is only so far we can go with our current resources," Vitomir said.

"Why don't you say anything?" Hicks asked.

Vitomir's eyebrows drew downward. "Because of what I've done to my Natalia and the others. My perspective on the state of your ship wouldn't be welcome," he said.

Hicks blew out a breath. The cosmonaut wasn't wrong.

"I would advise you to speak with Dr. Redford, but . . ." Vitomir began, leaving the thought unfinished.

Jonah Redford had succumbed to the Xiiginn compulsion, which effectively made him a sleeper agent for them. Hicks had gone over all the events that would have exposed Redford to the Xiiginn. They all had, and they'd determined that Redford's first exposure had been on the compound on Selebus. Redford had been unaccounted for for the span of a few minutes during the battle, and, according to the Boxans, a few moments was all that was required to plant the seed of compulsion in Jonah. Later on, during their escape from the Nershal star system, they'd received a strange transmission that they couldn't make sense of, and they'd overlooked it while they fled the system. Later, Kladomaor surmised that the signal had contained instructions for Jonah. The Xiiginns had gambled that Humans would be susceptible to their compulsion ability. They'd been right about Jonah but not about Zack, for some reason.

"Well, I want you to share those opinions of yours with me at the very least. Is that understood?" Hicks asked.

"Yes, Major."

They continued on, patching the Athena's hull where they could and noting other areas that would require further investigation. Hicks resolved himself to the fact that he needed to sit down with Kaylan and make a case for them to abandon this search for the Drars in order to return home to Earth while they still could.

CHAPTER THREE

K ladomaor sat on the command couch on the bridge of the Boxan stealth ship, reviewing the latest information from his neural feeds and feeling the grim lines of his face deepen into a tight frown. He was overdue for his mandatory time in the resonance chamber, a place for quiet meditation under a spectrum of light that some might fool themselves into believing was the star from their home system of Sethion. A pang resonated deep within him at the thought of the Boxan home world that had been lost to them. Their colony world was also a beautiful place but lacked the ancestral ties that formed the foundation of their species.

The door to the bridge hissed open and in walked a Nershal, a winged species with smooth, pale-green skin and deep orange eyes. The Nershals had once betrayed the Boxans to the Xiiginns but were now coming to the realization that the Xiiginns were not their allies. The Nershal walked straight to Kladomaor and bowed his head.

"Battle Commander, Ma'jasalax awaits you," Etanu said.

Kladomaor cut off his neural feeds and stood up. "Very well. Triflan, you have the bridge," Kladomaor said.

Triflan, his tactical officer, took his position at the command couch.

Etanu waited for Kladomaor to lead the way, as was proper. Kladomaor was the battle commander of this ship, and a hole opened up for him to walk through as the rest of the Boxan crew stepped to the side to allow him to pass. The Humans were much less formal on their ship, although if it had been a military vessel, Kladomaor suspected the protocol would be different. Dale Hicks left him with that impression.

It was good to move his limbs. He needed time in the starshine to truly center himself, but his duty to his crew demanded otherwise.

The smooth walls of the ship had been their home for a long time, but even they could not remain in the great expanse forever. At some point, they'd need to resupply. They were forbidden from returning to the Boxan colony world because one of the Human crewmembers was afflicted by the Xiiginn influence. If they tried to enter the colony space, their ship would be destroyed. Kladomaor would never abandon the Human ship to resupply, so there was that problem. No Boxan commander would resupply them as long as the Humans had a crewmember under the Xiiginn influence. Kladomaor knew that to the Humans these protocols seemed harsh, but the protocols had been established for a reason. Protecting what was left of the Boxans was paramount. Had those protocols been in place before, perhaps they wouldn't have lost their home world.

The great doors opened, and Kladomaor walked into the

conference room with Etanu trailing behind. Ma'jasalax was speaking with Gaarokk and Ezerah, and the Mardoxian priestess looked over at him as he joined them.

He looked at Gaarokk. "How are our wayward travelers doing?" Kladomaor asked.

"They tend to their ship as best they can," Gaarokk answered.

"They must realize their ship needs some time in a space dock. It was never meant for travel beyond the confines of their star system," Kladomaor said.

"I think we can agree on the stubbornness of Humans," Gaarokk said.

Ezerah shifted in her seat, her wings adjusting as well. "Wouldn't they come aboard this ship to seek refuge?"

Ma'jasalax cleared her throat. "Humans can be quite territorial. I'm sure they would if the Athena became unlivable, but for the time being, they'll be fine where they are."

"Territorial," Kladomaor said. "That's one way to put it."

"Like most intelligent species, they need to control their own destiny. They can accept help for a time, but they will never abandon their ship," Gaarokk said.

Kladomaor couldn't argue with the scientist. He made a good point, even if Kladomaor knew the Humans wouldn't be much safer aboard his ship.

"Having spent some time aboard their ship, I can vouch for its design. The Humans built an excellent ship, and given more time they would have expanded out into space on their own," Gaarokk said.

"Time is a luxury we can ill afford. In order for them to survive this journey, they simply need more than what they're capable of now," Kladomaor said.

Etanu cleared his throat. "If you felt that way, why did you let them come on this journey to begin with? Why not just take them back to their own star system?"

"The Xiiginns know about Humans now. Perhaps we *should* take them back to Earth and help them prepare for the Xiiginns," Kladomaor said.

Ma'jasalax released a great sigh. "We could do as you're suggesting. It was something I'd considered, but what they need, and us as well, is a way to turn the tide of this war with the Xiiginns. Since the war now affects Humans, they have a right to be here, and to be honest, I'm not sure we can succeed in finding the Drars without them."

Kladomaor swung his flaxen-eyed gaze toward the Mardoxian priestess. "Whose purpose is the Human presence really serving here then? Their own or yours?"

"Fate rarely chooses us on our own terms," Ma'jasalax replied.

"Fate, is it? It wasn't fate that sent the Mardoxian signal to the Human star system all those cycles ago," Kladomaor said.

The female Boxan stiffened. "You're in command of this ship. Do what you will, Battle Commander. Apparently you don't need or want my counsel."

Kladomaor planted his fist on the table and leaned forward. "I just want you to admit that you're influencing these events. You're operating outside the will of the Mardoxian Sect, which means you act without their consent."

Ma'jasalax's large ears twitched, which, for many Boxans, was a sign of annoyance. "I'm not the only one here who is acting outside the confines of command. Your efforts to ignite a rebellion in the Nershal star system weren't exactly sanctioned by the fleet."

Kladomaor chuckled, releasing some of the tension that had been building between them.

"You forget that Prax'pedax escaped the space station and should now be presenting our reports to the High Council about Humans. They won't stand idly by with the Mardoxian potential in Humans. They'll never hand that over to the Xiiginns, so the Humans are hardly abandoned to their fate," Ma'jasalax said.

Kladomaor looked away, considering.

"Kaylan is gifted, even by our standards. If her abilities can be further developed, and if there are more like her on Earth, Humans could become a formidable force in the galaxy," Ma'jasalax said.

Kladomaor leaned back in his chair. "By Gaarokk's account, Kaylan could be capable of much more than our most gifted Mardoxian priests."

"You imply more gifted than me. Do you think that bothers me?" Ma'jasalax asked.

"Does it?"

"No, it doesn't bother me. It's something I embrace."

"Be careful, or they might not look too kindly on the game you're playing," Kladomaor said.

"The game that allows both our species to survive against the Xiiginns? I'm doing what must be done."

"And so will I when the time comes," Kladomaor said.

The silence dragged between them, and Gaarokk cleared his throat. "We've found further evidence of the Drar, but the next jump will be a long one. This could be the one that takes us to the source of the signal."

"Very well," Kladomaor said. "Make sure the Athena knows."

"Actually, it was Zack who figured it out," Gaarokk said. "Well, him and their AI."

Kladomaor exchanged glances with Ma'jasalax but didn't say anything. Instead, he left them and headed for the resonance chamber. Perhaps a quiet meditation would do him some good.

CHAPTER FOUR

For the past few days, Edward Johnson had hardly left NORAD. He wasn't in custody per se, but it was frowned upon when he tried to leave. Regardless, this was where he needed to be for the moment. The original draft used for the proposal to form the Earth Coalition Force, or ECF, had been authored by many people, but it had been Bruce Matherson who put it together, and Ed had worked on an updated version prior to sending it to the White House, where it was being considered by some and outright dismissed by others in Halloway's cabinet. Regardless of what President Halloway decided, the ECF proposal would be brought to the other governments of the world. The ECF's greatest chance of success required the backing of the major superpowers of the Earth, despite evidence that the world was reluctant to believe it was in danger at all. Ed never underestimated some people's need to bury their heads in the sand and hope the problems facing them would simply go away. But they wouldn't go away. Not this time.

Ed had been at NASA Mission Control in Houston, Texas, for most of the communications with Michael Hunsicker. Besides the Athena crew, Michael was the only Human to have any dealings with a Boxan. Ed didn't care what species you were, no one would voluntarily stay in suspended animation, not even risking a call home, if they hadn't believed wholeheartedly that the Xiiginns were a real threat. Chazen, the Boxan left stranded on the dwarf planet Pluto, was such a being. The Xiiginns were coming, and they weren't coming for the betterment of humanity.

Ed walked through the underground network of hallways to the war room, and the clipped cadence of Iris's Louboutin heels followed him as they entered. He was a few minutes late, and the meeting had already started. One thing he could say about General Sheridan was that he ran a tight schedule. A ten thirty start time meant exactly that. Ed glanced over at General Sheridan. Over the past few days, he'd gotten the distinct impression that Sheridan viewed him as someone to be tolerated at the moment.

Gary Hunter's large, curly-haired head was on the wall screen. He glanced over at Ed as he took his seat. There was a momentary acknowledgment, and then he continued.

"The latest report from Armstrong Lunar Base is that the Endurance is in the final phases of construction and scheduled for routine stress tests by the end of the week. Test flights are scheduled for next week," Gary said.

General Sheridan glanced over at him, and Ed kept his facial features neutral. He'd already known the current status of the Endurance before coming to the meeting.

"That's excellent news," Dr. Philip Gray said. "I'm a bit

surprised you were able to finish construction so far ahead of schedule. We were under the impression that the aggressive schedule already established was a bit of a stretch."

Gary bobbed his head. "And you'd be right but for a couple of things. One, we've learned a few things since completing the Athena's construction. Two, the data provided on the Athena's performance was instrumental in design improvements. And, three, we've had input from Chazen."

Gray's beady eyes drew up in alarm. "I'd realized we were in near constant communications with Commander Hunsicker and the Boxan, Chazen, but I didn't think we were giving him access to the design of the Endurance."

Ed cleared his throat, and Sheridan gave him a nod to speak. "I was at Mission Control when this was discussed. The Endurance was being rushed to completion so it could be used to not only rescue Michael Hunsicker but Chazen as well. The Endurance is designed for Humans, and there was a need to consult with the Boxan on how best to transport him back to Earth. Chazen was quite reluctant to share any information because of the doctrines of his species, but Michael eventually convinced him of the advantage of at least having the option to leave Pluto when the Endurance got there."

Gray's mouth formed a circle but no words came out, and Ed once again wondered why in hell President Susan Halloway had appointed such an idiot as scientific advisor.

"Thank you, Mr. Hunter," General Sheridan said.

The wall screen flickered off, and Colonel Hines took the lead. The holodisplay above them came on and showed a scale model of the Endurance. It was the spitting image of the Athena but for the noticeable improvements and accommodations for the Boxan they planned to transport.

"Direct your attention to the holodisplay," Hines said. "As a reminder to all non-military personnel in the room, what is shown and discussed here is strictly confidential."

Ed frowned as he focused on the model of the Endurance. A duplicate image appeared but with modifications that conspicuously changed the spaceship intended for scientific exploration into something else entirely.

"The situation has changed," Hines said.

The sleek lines of the ship now had smaller towers on top and bottom. Ed focused on the updated legend that labeled each part of the ship and noticed that the large chambers designed for the Boxan had been changed.

Ed's eyebrows rose, and his gaze darted to Sheridan. "An armory? Missile towers?" he asked.

"That's right. The Endurance will no longer be a vessel for scientific research. Our engineers have been preparing these components as well and can easily retrofit the Endurance," Sheridan said.

Ed swallowed hard. "But Michael Hunsicker . . ."

"I'm afraid a rescue mission that will take the Endurance to Pluto is off the table," Sheridan said.

Ed felt as if he'd been punched in the stomach. He should have anticipated this. The military had allowed the Endurance's construction to go along, with the plan of commandeering the vessel when it was completed.

"General, please reconsider this. Chazen could be a valuable asset—" Ed started to say.

"I don't like this any more than you do. If we had another

ship like the Endurance, I'd send it out there to bring Michael Hunsicker home, but the risk of losing such an important ship for one man in a time such as this . . . The risk is too great."

Ed's mind raced. There was no way Sheridan could do this on his own. These orders had come down from the top, and that meant President Halloway had signed off on them. Michael Hunsicker, the former commander of the Athena, was on his own. Ed drew in a breath and slowly released it. It twisted him up inside, but Ed knew Sheridan and the president were right.

Sheridan watched him and waited for him to come to the only conclusion he could. Ed wished there were something he could do for Hunsicker. He was a good man and didn't deserve what was going to happen to him. Ed wanted to argue for sending the Endurance anyway, but the shrewd part of his brain knew it wouldn't change the facts. The Xiiginns were coming, and they needed every resource available for the defense of Earth.

"Now that we're on the same page, it's time we turned our attention to the inventory of space vehicles we have that can be used in our defense," Sheridan said.

Ed glanced at the small console in front of him as the rest of the meeting's agenda came into prominence, the next line item highlighted. At least they were taking the threat seriously, but Ed still would have liked to bring Hunsicker back home.

CHAPTER FIVE

Billions of miles from Earth, in a small Boxan outpost on the dwarf planet Pluto, Commander Michael Hunsicker gazed at the amber holodisplay, which showed a feed from outside the outpost. Flakes of methane gently fell to Pluto's icy surface. If Michael let himself, he could almost imagine he was back on Earth, looking out the window of his house in Boulder, Colorado. He closed his eyes and imagined the cool granite countertops in the kitchen with the smell of Irish breakfast tea brewing in two mugs on the countertop. Across from his kitchen were large, two-story windows with a picturesque view of the Rocky Mountain foothills.

Michael felt a sharp pang twist in his chest as the memory of his home faded. Kathryn had passed away four years before, and he still missed her fiercely, but he resigned himself to the fact that he always would miss his wife. Some part of him must have thought that going on the Athena mission would put distance between himself and his grief, but being stranded on Pluto had brought the mourning of his dead wife to the forefront of his thoughts. Kathryn would have told him to pay attention to what he was doing, so that's what Michael was doing—solve one problem at a time, making the best decisions he could, and maybe he could get back home.

A bitter chuckle escaped his lips, drawing Chazen's attention. Michael had just received the latest update from Mission Control. Despite the spaceship Endurance nearing completion, the rescue mission had been delayed, but the update had been immediately followed by a video message from Edward Johnson, who gave him a more realistic view.

"There's no easy way tell you this, so I'm just going to say it . . ."

The Endurance wasn't coming. There would be no rescue mission for him. Michael sat down and felt his strength slowly ebb away. He'd been living on the hope of going home, and now that was being taken away from him.

Michael looked over at Chazen. When he stood, the Boxan was ten feet tall, with brown, roughened skin and eyes the size of giant teacups.

"You don't seem surprised," Michael said.

"No, not after we got the update from your crew."

Eight weeks ago they'd finally received the update from the Athena that had shocked the world. Michael had watched video logs of each of the crew. He was delighted that they were still alive but horrified at what they'd discovered. He'd always known Kaylan would make an excellent commander. He reviewed her logs and updates and doubted that he could have done any better. In fact, he felt that she had surpassed him as commander. If there was anything his astronaut career had taught him, it was that things could change quickly, and if you couldn't adapt, the price of failure may very well be paid with your life.

"I thought that since the Endurance was so close to being completed there was still time for a rescue mission," Michael said.

"That was before. Now they're starting to believe the Xiiginns may actually find this star system," Chazen said.

Michael looked away from the Boxan for a moment. "If the Xiiginns come here in force, is there anything we can do to stop them?" he asked.

"As I've told you before, I'm not a soldier. I'm not sure—"

"Take a guess then," Michael interrupted.

Chazen regarded him for a long moment. "No, you couldn't stop them."

Michael squeezed his hand, forming a fist, and bounced it on the desktop. "I refuse to accept that. There has to be something we can do. Isn't there anything you can share with us that will give us a fighting chance?"

The sharp lines of Chazen's face deepened, but the Boxan remained silent.

"Can't we try again to reach out to your species?" he pressed.

"No, Kladomaor confirmed that Sethion is unreachable, and he wouldn't disclose where our colony was located. So there's nowhere I could send a message," Chazen answered.

Michael stood up. "We can't just wait around here and do nothing."

"There is always stasis. I've worked out how to adapt a pod for your use," Chazen offered.

Michael shook his head. "No, I can't sleep my life away and neither should you. You've done more than your duty to the

Boxans. We need to focus on figuring out a way to get to Earth. If they won't come to us, then we need to go to them."

Michael paced a few steps, trying to think of a way, and an idea blazed into his mind. He turned back to Chazen.

"There are no ships here and no means to build one. We have no way to get to Earth," Chazen said.

Michael smiled. "We don't need a ship. Just hear me out."

Chazen said he would.

"What we need is a life pod, ideally something with limited maneuvering capability in zero gravity and comms capability. We need to be able to live aboard for a certain amount of time . . ." Michael's voice trailed off. "We'll figure that out later."

"What good will a life pod do? It's not a ship. It can't take you to your planet," Chazen said.

"We don't need it to. We just need to get it off the surface of Pluto. This place has the power to create a wormhole. The AI did it. I know you said the power requirements almost drained the reserves here, but we only need to put the pod in the vicinity of Earth," Michael said, his voice rising in excitement.

Chazen shook his head. "It's much too dangerous. Even Cherubian drives open wormholes only at the edge of a star system. Otherwise, it affects navigation."

"I'm not talking about pinpointing a place somewhere in the galaxy," Michael said, flinging his arm out for emphasis. "I'm talking something much smaller. I think if we could get closer to Earth, they wouldn't have a choice but to come get us."

"You would risk this?" Chazen asked.

"Not alone. I'd want you to come with me."

Chazen's bushy brows lifted. "I appreciate the sentiment, but I cannot leave."

"You cannot stay. If the Xiiginns . . . *when* the Xiiginns come here, where do you think they'll come first?"

Michael watched as Chazen considered. The Boxans were a stubborn race.

"If you stay here, you'd be effectively throwing your life away, and that's not something even your High Council would want. There is a way. We can do this with everything here. We *have* to be able to do this," Michael said.

"When the Xiiginns come, I will set the self-destruct to prevent them from gaining access to the shroud network," Chazen said.

"Fine," Michael said. "Set it and come with me to Earth."

The Boxan looked away from him. It was moments like these that reminded Michael of how alone Chazen must feel. He'd been trapped here for over sixty years and had no way to get home. Michael had only had a taste of that, and it was enough to drive him to do whatever he could do to get home again.

Chazen came to his feet but didn't say anything. Michael knew the Boxan was using his neural feeds because the holoscreens nearby flickered to life, and it took Michael's own implants a few moments to translate the information on the holoscreens. Chazen had brought up an inventory and begun highlighting certain things on the list. Michael glanced over at the Boxan and felt his chest begin to swell. Perhaps there was a way for them to get home after all.

CHAPTER SIX

K aylan Farrow glanced out the forward windows on the bridge of the Athena. An ocean of stars shined with a brilliance that seemed to stretch to infinity. With the help of the Boxans, they'd traveled farther into space than any Human before. While they now knew their position in relation to Earth, she knew that not even the Boxans had equipment capable of allowing them to see their home star system.

Her long brown hair had a slight curl to it, and she absently ran her fingers through it. There was always more to see. She'd gazed up at the night sky on Earth, wondering what it would be like to travel among the stars, visiting other planets, but since they'd been snatched from Earth's star system, they'd hardly had a moment to enjoy it—hardly a moment to take a breath and simply be in the moment.

She'd found comfort with the other crewmembers, especially Zack, but they could hardly flaunt their relationship. Discretion was something both she and Zack easily agreed on. She glanced over at Zack, who sat at the communications station, muttering at the holoscreens in front of him, and the edges of her lips curved upward. Zack liked to talk things out while he worked, even when he was alone. It was something she'd first noticed when they were at MIT together and was a habit he hadn't lost over the years.

A loud crash sounded as several stacks of metal containers hit the floor, and Zack was on his feet instantly, scanning the area for any sign of danger. He blinked several times before he settled back down and tried to give her a reassuring wave. That behavior was new. This ready-for-danger-at-a-moment's-notice reaction was something Zack hadn't done until he'd been captured and held prisoner by the Xiiginns. He hardly spoke of his sojourn in the pit, but Etanu had told her enough. Kaylan had hoped that with enough time Zack could distance himself from such a horrible place, but apparently it was too soon. She wished he'd confide in her about it.

Emma Roberson called out an apology while she collected the fallen containers and stacked them again. Kaylan hastened over to her and was lending a hand when the door to the bridge opened and Dale Hicks walked in with Vitomir on his heels. Hicks headed over to them.

"The micro-fractures are getting worse," Hicks said.

"We have enough repair kits for the time being, and Klado-maor can send us more if we need them," Kaylan replied.

"And what if something happens to them? We're becoming too dependent on the Boxans. I'm worried that we could be left stranded out here," Hicks said.

Zack stood up and came over to them, his hand rubbing the

back of his neck. "It's not like Kladomaor would just leave us out here."

Hicks shook his head. "Of course not. I'm just trying to mitigate risk here, consider things that no one else is willing to talk about."

Here it comes again, Kaylan thought.

"We've been over this. We even discussed it with Kladomaor and the others. If something catastrophic were to happen to the Athena, we would go aboard their ship," Kaylan said.

"Not good enough," Hicks said. "We're ignoring the fact that we're taking the Athena to places she wasn't designed to go."

Zack frowned. "It's a spaceship, and this is space. What else is there?"

"Did you forget the binary pulsar we encountered a few weeks ago? We all almost died within minutes of arriving, not to mention the damage to the electrical systems," Hicks said.

Zack glanced at Kaylan, cocking his head to the side and raising his hands.

"We knew there were risks when we came along," Kaylan said.

Hicks nodded. "Finding the Drar, which will hopefully lead us to something that will help turn the tide of the war with the Xiiginns. The thing is that officially we're not at war with the Xiiginns yet."

"What are you saying?" Kaylan asked.

"I'm saying we should consider returning to Earth and bringing a bigger team that is better able to deal with the rigors this type of mission incurs."

"You mean more military," Zack said.

Hicks nodded. "And more specialists like all of you. We've

cross-trained for various jobs as best we can, but there are only so many of us. And if something happens to Kladomaor, we have no hope of ever getting back home."

Kaylan understood all the risks Hicks was identifying, and each and every one of them was right, but deep down in her gut she knew Earth's future would be affected by what they did out here. The thing was, she had no sound reasoning for believing as she did. Hicks wouldn't hold it against her, but logic would dictate that his sound reasoning was a much better argument than her gut instinct.

"Athena," Zack said. "What's the probability of survival should we lose our Boxan friends along the way?"

"There are multiple variables that could affect the odds of survival, which I can estimate, but on the highest level, the odds of your survival would be zero without help from the Boxans," the AI said.

"Is there anything we could do to increase the odds of our survival?" Zack asked.

"There are a number of enhancements to this spacecraft that could be done but all would require more resources than are currently available to you."

"When you say resources, is it something the Boxans could help us with or something we could find?" Hicks asked.

"To greatly increase the odds of survival, you would need to install a Cherubian drive and higher-grade hull plating—"

"Thank you," Kaylan said, cutting the AI off. "We can't build a new ship out here. I think we just need a little more time, and if we find no sign of the Drars, I'll ask Kladomaor to take us back to Earth."

Hicks pressed his lips together, considering. "Okay," he said and glanced at Zack. "What have you got on this new signal?"

Zack sighed. "I really could use Redford's expertise, but he's not exactly in his right mind."

"What's the problem?"

"The signal is intermittent but almost seems random. I'm not sure if it's artificial in nature. I wouldn't have even spotted it if it weren't for Athena. Even Gaarokk doesn't know what to make of it until we get closer," Zack said.

"Another jump then," Hicks said.

Kaylan nodded.

"Have you or Ma'jasalax been able to detect anything?" Hicks asked.

"She hasn't," Kaylan said.

Hicks regarded her with a raised brow.

Kaylan shook her head and rolled her eyes. "I just have a feeling that where we detected that signal is where we need to go. It's nothing else. Just a feeling."

Hicks pressed his lips together. "You also knew Zack was still alive even when the rest of us weren't so sure. I'd say your instincts are trustworthy enough for us to stay out here longer."

Kaylan smiled. "Thank you," she said.

Hicks had turned out to be a good friend, and she counted on his support. He could lay out his thoughts and present the risks but was willing to take a leap of faith just the same. She hoped they wouldn't regret it.

CHAPTER SEVEN

Mar Arden stood on the bridge of a Xiiginn warship at a Confederation space station. The massive station had been built and then expanded by the different species that formed the Confederation, but the structure was originally designed by the Boxans, even though the founding members of the Confederation had been cast out. The space station was essentially an artificial planetoid space dock, protected by a massive shield with an artificial atmosphere that most species could breathe.

The Boxans had only made contact with species that were able to thrive in similar atmospheres. The Xiiginns knew the Boxans were aware of other species out there, but that knowledge had been locked away from them and was one of the driving forces behind finding an intact Star Shroud system. Gaining access to a shroud network would allow them to find other species that the Boxans had deemed unworthy of the Confederation. Cultivating the uprising that had led to the downfall of the

Boxans had been a delicate operation, carried out with precision and tact; otherwise, the species of the Confederation would have turned against them. Mar Arden knew there were species biding their time, waiting for the opportune moment to strike, but for them there would be no opportune moment. The Xiiginn fleets were the most advanced force in the galaxy. The only species that could stand against them had cut themselves off on a colony world. Mar Arden would have loved to find the Boxan colony world and extinguish their race from the great expanse but had to date been unsuccessful in those efforts.

Mar Arden glanced over at the command couch occupied by Hoan Berend, the Xiiginn captain, who waved him over. Mar Arden blew out a breath before joining the captain.

"We have orders to find the star system that's home to the Humans," Hoan Berend said.

Mar Arden's tail flicked in annoyance. "What about my request to pursue Kladomaor?"

Hoan Berend frowned. "Denied. The Boxans are going to great lengths to keep knowledge of the Humans away from us. Finding their home star system is of the utmost priority."

Mar Arden frowned. "There are other battle groups that could do this."

"The orders came from Supreme Leader Garm Antis himself. Once the system has been identified, he has already designated an attack force to go to that system."

"And the Confederation?" Mar Arden asked.

"They are to be kept ignorant of this species. The Nershals have petitioned for a grievance with the Confederation for the events that transpired in their star system," Hoan Berend said.

"I don't expect much to come of that."

Hoan Berend studied him for a moment. "You don't want to pursue the Humans?"

"Of course I do, but I want Kladomaor as well. The Boxans are up to something. They didn't put resources into an asteroid base for no reason. Why would they possibly return to the Qegi star system?"

"That I couldn't say. Our orders are to go back to the Nershal star system to find evidence of the wormhole the Humans used to get there," Hoan Berend said.

"Send one of your other ships," Mar Arden said.

Hoan Berend looked slightly amused. "I'm not going to defy Garm Antis for you. If he says that's where we're supposed to go, then that is exactly where I shall take you."

Mar Arden clenched his teeth but knew it was useless. Hoan Berend wouldn't deviate from his orders. "What about sending another ship to investigate the Qegi star system and figure out where Kladomaor and the others escaped to?" Mar Arden asked.

Hoan Berend's fingertips grazed the control panel on his armrest. "I think we could spare a scout ship for that."

Mar Arden supposed he should be thankful for that much, at least. Responsibility for the events that had taken place in the Nershal star system was being placed on his shoulders—rather, the powers that be were trying to hold him responsible, but Mar Arden hadn't attained his position by playing by the rules. Garm Antis would expect that. The question remaining was how far he could push things before they spiraled beyond his control.

CHAPTER EIGHT

Zack climbed down from the top observatory. Sometimes he just needed to escape the bridge and find a quiet place to think. Since Jonah Redford was confined to quarters, Zack had taken it upon himself to ensure that the astrophysicist's work continued. All that stuff Hicks kept bringing up about the current state of the Athena had him worried, and Zack was committed to using the AI to help address some of those issues, but there was only so much they could do. The onboard fabricators had the capacity to replace internal components of the ship, but there were limits, and the AI had a haunting way of pointing out the cold hard facts. Zack had asked her to be more tactful when it came to delivering unsettling news pertaining to things like zero percent chance of survival. That was one of his favorites. He'd lost count of how many different ways they could die out here, and as Kaylan liked to point out to him, it wasn't healthy to constantly dwell on worst-case scenarios.

Zack gave a mental shake of his head and blew out a harsh

breath. Truth be told, without the AI they probably wouldn't have made it as far as they had. The AI wasn't infallible and couldn't account for things like Kaylan's psychic abilities, which it classified as an unknown quantity, and Zack supposed that was correct. How else could something that was unknowable be accounted for? Sometimes the insights Kaylan had were downright creepy. He couldn't figure out how she could do the things she did. A couple of times they'd plotted a course and at the last second Kaylan had called for a course correction that ended up sparing the ship from running into trouble, but Ma'jasalax had informed them that this was quite normal and that they should trust Kaylan's instincts.

Zack headed back toward the bridge, making a quick stop to grab a protein pack and refill his water bottle. He didn't have time for anything else, and while the protein pack tasted like cardboard, it would stave off hunger for a couple of hours. Stuffing the bar into his mouth and chewing vigorously, he headed toward the bridge.

Kaylan and Hicks occupied the pilot seats, and he headed over to the comms station. Katie Garcia was already there and glanced up at his approach.

"Took you long enough," Katie said.

"I had to get something to eat on the way here. I was starving," Zack said.

Katie nodded and shifted her attention to the holoscreens in front of her.

Zack took his seat. "Comms is a go," he said.

The rest of the crew checked in from their designated work areas. Efren and Nikolai were in Engineering, Brenda and Emma were in the hydroponics lab, and Redford was confined to his room, sleeping, since Brenda had recommended that he be sedated for these high-risk maneuvers. Vitomir monitored one of the consoles on the bridge. They were green across the board. The status indicator showed that the gravity tether from the Boxan stealth ship was in place. A small progress bar appeared on their screens, showing the Cherubian drive powering up. Zack hated this part. Whenever they went through a wormhole, he always felt a bit nauseous on the other side. But the idiom of 'the other side' wasn't quite right. There was no other side. The Cherubian drive allowed them to fold space in such a way that enabled them to cross vast distances quickly. They'd done this five other times, and it still grated on Zack's nerves.

"Focus, Zack," Katie said.

Zack glanced over at her and nodded. He was glad they'd remained friends. He hadn't been sure there for a while and had kept his distance from Katie, but she had called him out on it. The Athena wasn't that big, and there was no way for them to avoid one another.

Zack experienced a sudden craving for a pint of Guinness beer. He couldn't remember the last time he'd had a drink and found that he could use one right about now. No such luck though. NASA hadn't stocked the Athena with any alcoholic beverages. Even Hunsicker's stash was gone.

"Maybe it won't be so bad this time," Zack muttered.

"Fail-safe for tether active," Hicks called out.

"Acknowledged," Kaylan said.

The fail-safe was something new that allowed them to instantly reverse the gravity field that kept the tether in place in case of an emergency. Kaylan had told him they'd done such a thing before when Kladomaor attempted to force the Athena to leave the Nershal star system without Zack. He didn't hold this attempt against the Boxan. Kladomaor was doing what he thought was right, but he was glad Kaylan and the rest of the crew hadn't left without him.

As they approached the jump point, Zack had the feeling there was some unseen force pulling him forward, stretching him to infinity. It reminded him of riding a rollercoaster as it pulled over the apex of the first major drop, but instead of the feeling of dropping waaaaaayyyyyy down lasting for a few seconds, jumping through space and time lasted much longer.

They entered the wormhole, and Zack felt his insides twist up in anticipation as he tried to calm down. On his internal heads-up display, he brought up an image of Kaylan sitting in the commander's seat. He'd done this during the last two jumps, and it had really helped. He focused in on her face, but instead of the calming effect he'd anticipated, he felt his heart sink to his feet. Her forehead was creased in worry, and her lips were pale. Her eyes seemed to take in the readouts on her holoscreen and focus on something beyond at the same time. She didn't look relaxed as she normally did during a jump. Zack swallowed hard and grabbed onto the arms of his chair just as everything went to hell.

CHAPTER NINE

K ladomaor sat on the command couch on the bridge of
the ship. The couch was located on an elevated platform
in the center of the bridge, which allowed him to view the other
workstations. Engaging the Cherubian drive to a set of coordinates was a routine procedure that carried relatively little risk.
When the alarms began blaring, the Boxans on the bridge were
caught in a moment of surprise.

"Status report," Kladomaor barked.

Varek, his navigation officer, hunched over his console.
"Wormhole is unstable, Battle Commander."

"What's causing it?"

"Unknown—"

The ship shook violently, and Kladomaor grabbed onto his
seat. "Abort the jump."

"The system is unresponsive. We're locked in," Varek said.

Kladomaor used his neural link to execute the abort order,
but the Cherubian drive wouldn't respond. He looked at

Ma'jasalax, and the entire bridge went dark. There were several loud pops just outside the bridge, and Kladomaor felt himself rise into the air as the gravity field anchoring them to the floor became disabled. Emergency lighting came on as they automatically went to auxiliary power.

Kladomaor opened a comms channel to Engineering from his suit computer. "Situation report," he said.

The rest of the Boxans on the bridge pulled themselves back to their consoles.

"The main reactor is down, Commander, as well as the primary auxiliary power source. Emergency life support only."

Kladomaor's mind raced. Total loss of power aboard a Boxan starship never happened. He used his suit computer to bring up a damage report.

"What's the status of the Athena?" Ma'jasalax asked.

"Unknown," Triflan answered. "My station is dark. Switching to suit computer."

Boxan warships had built-in redundancies in the event of power loss or systems failure. Critical systems were capable of running on auxiliary or emergency power, but in order to handle the switch, each critical system had its own limited power source. To get the current status of the ship, Kladomaor had to access each critical system one by one. The more systems he couldn't access, the more he realized they were in real trouble. Someone or something had completely disabled his ship. They were adrift in the great expanse. He accessed the short-range communications array and tried to contact the Athena, but there was no response.

"See if you can detect the Athena nearby," Kladomaor said.

Triflan went to work for a few moments. "They're not there."

"What do you mean 'not there'?" Ma'jasalax said. "The gravity tether should have held. Are all our sensors out?"

Triflan shook his head. "They are, but even if the Athena only had life support, they would still emit an energy signature that our short-range sensors could detect. I'm telling you, they aren't there."

Ma'jasalax looked at Kladomaor in alarm, and the battle commander drew in a determined breath.

"Focus," Kladomaor said. "We need to assess the damage and get primary power back online first. Then we'll worry about finding the Athena."

Ma'jasalax frowned. "We can't have lost them. What could cause a wormhole to destabilize like that?"

"We won't be able to determine that until power is restored," Kladomaor said.

Ma'jasalax closed her eyes for a moment, and her brow smoothed in concentration. After a few seconds, she opened her eyes. "I can't find them."

Kladomaor frowned. "What do you mean? I thought you had a Mardoxian connection to Kaylan."

"I do, but it's simply not there anymore," Ma'jasalax said, and her brows drew up in fear. "It's as if something is blocking the connection."

"Varek, you're with me; Triflan, you have the bridge," Kladomaor said. He needed to check the ship and work his way down to Engineering. "They probably disengaged the gravity tether at the first sign of trouble and were safely deposited from the wormhole. We'll find them, but first we need figure out what happened and what shape we're in."

Kladomaor waved two more crew members over to follow

him, and Etanu also came over as he reached the doors. The Nershal's suit had magnetic boots that had kicked on as soon as they lost gravity.

"Put me to work, Battle Commander," Etanu said.

"Follow me," Kladomaor replied and left the bridge.

CHAPTER TEN

The blinking lights of the Athena's dashboard went from blurry to razor-sharp focus as Kaylan regained full consciousness. She was slumped forward against her seat belt, and the straps were digging into her ribs. Master alarms sounded, and she pushed herself upright, glancing over at Hicks, who was slowly regaining consciousness. She looked back at the systems-failure listing on the main holoscreen. They still had life support. Kaylan unbuckled her seat belt and climbed out of the chair. Hicks looked a bit disoriented but was otherwise okay. She looked over at the comms station for Zack, whose sagging form slouched in his chair. Her stomach clenched, and she ran over to him, calling out his name. Zack's eyes snapped open, and he sucked in a breath.

"You're okay," Kaylan told him.

Katie was checking herself for injuries and finding none. "I'm all right," she said.

"Good. We need to check on the others," Kaylan said.

She looked over to the other side of the bridge and saw Vitomir regaining consciousness.

"Athena, status report," Kaylan said.

"Multiple systems failure, Commander."

"What's the status of the rest of the crew?" Kaylan asked.

"I'm detecting three life signs in the hydroponics laboratory," the AI said.

"What about Efren and Nikolai in Engineering?" Kaylan asked.

There was a heavy moment of silence while she was waiting for the AI to answer her.

"Apologies, Commander, I'm not able to detect any life signs in Engineering."

Kaylan gasped, her mouth agape in horror for a moment before her training forced her to focus, to keep assessing and avoid making assumptions.

"Is there life support in Engineering?"

"Apologies, Commander, but it seems that the sensors in the engineering area are offline."

Zack came over to her. "What about exterior sensors outside the fusion reactor?" he asked.

"Exterior sensors report no damage. It is unlikely there are any hull breaches in that area," the AI reported.

Hicks joined them. "We're unable to get the status of several other sections of the ship besides Engineering."

"Right, we'll need to check each area then," Kaylan said and walked over to a storage locker on the wall. She retrieved three breather masks and handed them to Hicks, Katie, and Vitomir.

"Won't I need one of those?" Zack asked, sticking his hand out.

Kaylan shook her head. "I need you to stay on the bridge."

"To do what? I could help you," Zack insisted.

Kaylan glanced at the others. "Can you give us a moment?" she said and led Zack away.

Zack's gaze bored into her intently.

"I need you to stay on the bridge and help coordinate from here. You're best at getting the AI to help us with what we need."

Zack pressed his lips together. "That's bullshit."

Kaylan hardened her tone. "You're right; it is. The others have extensive training for this kind of thing and you don't. Hicks and Katie have done salvage and repair, and Vitomir . . ." She had no choice but to utilize the cosmonaut, and she didn't need to point out Vitomir's qualifications to Zack. "I have to go. But it's not all bullshit. Find a way to help us from here."

Zack blew out a frustrated breath and nodded.

Kaylan joined the others. It wasn't that she wouldn't risk Zack. They'd all taken some measure of risk by going on this mission. As the commander, she had to utilize her resources where they could have maximum benefit, and that put Zack here on the bridge whether he liked it or not.

She slipped her breather mask over her face and attached the unit to her belt. The others waited for her by the door. The breather wouldn't help them if they got sucked out into space, but it would allow them to breathe in the event of a fuel leak or some other chemical that might have gotten mixed into the atmosphere.

"Slow and steady," Kaylan said.

She checked the panel on the door and opened it. They walked through, and the door to the bridge shut behind them.

"Athena, lock the bridge door," Kaylan said.

Hicks chuckled. "He's going to love that."

The lights in the corridor flickered for a moment and then stabilized. They needed to get down to Engineering first.

Kaylan opened a comms channel to the hydroponics lab. "Brenda, are you guys okay?"

"We're fine, Commander. Zack just informed us that you're heading down to Efren," Brenda said.

"That's right. The sensors are out, and we're not sure what's going on. I need you to meet us with your med kit," Kaylan said.

"I'll meet you there, Commander."

"Containment measures are in effect."

"Copy that," Brenda said.

Vitomir cleared his throat. "Containment measures?" he asked.

"It's why we're wearing breathers and checking the rooms as we go along. With sensors offline, I don't want to take any chances," Kaylan said.

Kaylan led them through the ship. Once the wormhole had become unstable, Athena had closed all doors as a preventative measure to contain any breaches or fires. If the sensors detected a fire, the fire suppression system would work to put it out, and the fact that the sensors were offline in Engineering didn't bode well that they were safe just because they'd made it out of the wormhole. Each door had to be checked. To save time, she sent Katie to check the port observatory and mess hall while Hicks and Vitomir followed her down to Engineering.

They reached the long yellow ladder that would be the most direct path down to where Efren worked. The hatch was shut. She checked the system indicator and it was out, but she was able to open the hatch, which she wouldn't have been able to do if there had been a hull breach. Beyond the hatch, tracks of orange emergency lighting were on. Kaylan stepped out onto the ladder and began to climb down, lights flickering as she went. When she reached the bottom, she stepped away from the ladder.

"Zack, can you hear me?" Kaylan asked into her comms unit.

"Loud and clear," Zack said.

"We have emergency lighting here. Do any of the readouts for the area show systems with an overload status?" Kaylan asked.

"One minute," Zack answered.

Hicks and Vitomir joined her. The central computer where the brain of the Athena resided was off to the left, but the main reactor room was to the right.

"Yeah, the main . . . all have a status of overload. I guess that stuff is on a different system than the atmospheric sensors," Zack said.

"Thanks," Kaylan said and looked at Hicks and Vitomir. "Sounds like if we put the main breakers back into position, we can restore primary power to the ship."

"Yeah, but why wouldn't Efren or Nikolai have already done that?" Hicks asked.

They slowly made their way down the darkened hallway, the inadequate emergency lighting augmented by Hicks's flashlight. There was no power in the control room, and it was dark. Kaylan grabbed the latch and was able to unlock the door. If they'd had a hull breach in this section, she wouldn't have been able to do that either. Vitomir stepped beside her and helped pull the door open. There was a soft hiss of air.

"Trace toxins detected, Commander," Vitomir said.

"Radiation levels are climbing," Hicks said.

Kaylan peered into the room. "Shine your light over there to the left."

Hicks's flashlight beam swept immediately to the side, and there, next to a table by two overturned chairs, were Efren and Nikolai. Kaylan raced to the storage locker and grabbed two breathers, fitting them over the unconscious men's faces.

Kaylan spotted the breakers and used her neural implants to double-check the procedure for putting the overloaded breakers back into position. Her HUD outlined the correct order, and she had to use both hands to push the large breakers back into position. She then moved to the main power relay and switched it back on.

The lights immediately came back up as main power was restored. She glanced up, noting the dark, burned-out areas. The overload must have fried the sensors, and it must have happened so fast that they didn't have time to register the failure. That shouldn't have been possible.

With main power restored, the atmospheric scrubbers cleaned the trace toxins from the air. They carried Efren and Nikolai from the control room because the radiation levels were a bit higher than normal. They'd have to keep an eye on it, as well as replace the sensors that had burned out.

Brenda checked them for injuries, and then they carried Efren and Nikolai to the sick bay. Both men were suffering from minor oxygen deprivation.

"Putting the breathers on helped," Brenda said.

She gave each of them a shot, and in few moments both men regained consciousness.

Efren rubbed his head and groaned. "My head is killing me," he said.

"Don't try to get up," Brenda said. "I can give you something for the pain."

Efren lay back and closed his eyes, waiting for the pain meds to kick in.

"Can you tell us what happened?" Kaylan asked when Efren opened his eyes again.

"It was strange. System indicators were reporting instability in the reactor core. The last thing I remember was going into the control room, and then there was this massive power surge," Efren said, and his face twisted into a confused frown.

"What is it?" Kaylan asked.

"It could be the bump on my head, but I could swear the power surge came from outside the ship and that's what threw the reactor core into disarray."

Kaylan nodded.

Efren sat up on the bed.

"What do you think you're doing?" Brenda asked.

"I can't afford to lay here. I have to check the reactor and the rest of Engineering," Efren said.

"You need to rest," Brenda said.

Efren smiled at the doctor. "If you're so concerned, you can come with me to make sure I'm okay."

Brenda rolled her eyes and looked at Kaylan pleadingly.

"We need to repair any damage to the ship and then figure out where we are," Kaylan said.

"He's had a head injury."

"I know, but we're all we have. Keep an eye on him then," Kaylan said.

Kaylan left the med bay, and Zack opened up a comms channel to her.

"Don't make me hack this door, Kaylan."

She chuckled. "Oh, sorry about that," Kaylan said and sent the release code for the door to the bridge.

The crew of the Athena went about the tasks of assessing the damage, and more than one of them noted how lucky they'd been, but Kaylan didn't believe in luck. There were too many strange occurrences for these events to be purely accidental.

With main power restored, damage assessments went quickly. It wasn't until they failed to detect Kladomaor's ship that they realized they were stranded out in deep space.

"Holy crap! We're all alone out here," Zack said.

They'd returned to the bridge and gathered around the conference table.

"I still don't understand what happened," Hicks said. "How'd we end up where we are?"

"Athena," Zack said. "Can you display the events right before things went wrong with the wormhole?"

"Of course," the AI said.

A list of events from launch prep to when they'd first entered the wormhole appeared normal. Kaylan read the list with everyone else.

"System override?" Zack asked as he read through the list. "It says here that the tether was released by you, Kaylan."

Kaylan frowned in thought, trying to remember how the events had unfolded. "The wormhole was becoming unstable."

"That's right, but not until thirty seconds later. We were patched into the Boxan ship's systems so we'd be able to see the status of the jump," Zack said.

Hicks rubbed his chin. "How'd you know the wormhole would become unstable?"

Kaylan shook her head. "I didn't. It was unstable to start with."

She looked at the logs, and somehow she'd known the wormhole had become unstable before the Boxan ship's computers did.

"Might I posit a theory, Commander?" the AI asked.

Kaylan rubbed the back of her neck. "Go ahead."

"If logic cannot provide a satisfactory explanation, then we must consider that there were outside forces that influenced these events."

"Meaning the power surge?" Kaylan said.

"Precisely, but the fact that your intuition gave you an insight into what was about to happen was remarkable, even by Mardoxian standards," the AI said.

"Yeah, but I don't even recall having the thought. I just acted," Kaylan said.

Zack's eyes lit up. "I get it. I know what the AI is trying to say. It was the 'outside forces' that kept tripping me up. The Boxans revere those with a strong Mardoxian trait. I've been reviewing the data we retrieved from the space station about the Drar, and there's a connection there. What if someone or something caused this to happen and sent you a message somehow?"

Kaylan considered what Zack said for a moment. "It wasn't anything like communicating with Ma'jasalax, and wouldn't she get the same message?"

Zack shrugged. "I don't pretend to understand how you're able to do what you can do. Are you able to contact Ma'jasalax now?"

Kaylan's brows furrowed in concentration for a moment, and then she shook her head. "Nothing at all."

"Sounds crazy, but I think we should pursue this," Zack said.

"How?" Kaylan asked.

"We're on the trail of the Drar, and we already knew we were getting close to them. Perhaps this all means something," Zack said and waved his hands, gesturing around them.

"It could be a warning to stay away," Hicks said.

"If this disaster was intentional, they could have killed us, but they didn't," Zack said.

"We should try to find Kladomaor," Hicks said.

"I agree," Kaylan said. Zack started to protest, but Kaylan interrupted him. "I think you're onto something, so I want you to pursue it, but in the meantime, we need to find Kladomaor."

She sounded confident, but what Zack said had alarmed her. No one wanted to broach the subject of what they would do if they couldn't find the Boxans.

CHAPTER ELEVEN

M ar Arden sat in his chambers aboard a Xiiginn warship. He would put on a display of cunning brilliance later on for Hoan Berend so the commander could report back to Garm Antis of his cooperation. Eventually he would challenge the supreme leader to his seat among the upper echelons of the Xiiginns, but not now. He simply didn't have the backing he required for that, and the loss of the Nershals had set his efforts back. Mar Arden was still First Ambassador, which officially made Hoan Berend, the commander of this squadron, his inferior, but the commander had made it quite clear that he would carry out Garm Antis's orders to the letter. Mar Arden wasn't worried about Hoan Berend. The commander was a means to an end, and eventually Mar Arden would offset the status quo back to his favor.

After he'd calmed his anger and distanced himself from his immediate wants, he'd realized that hunting the Humans to their home system would eventually lead him to Kladomaor and Zack

Quick. He hadn't forgotten the Human who had escaped from Kandra Rene on Selebus's moon. He wanted to unlock all the secrets the Humans had to offer, and he had no doubt that he would find their home star system.

The door to his chambers chimed.

"Enter."

Kandra Rene walked into his chambers, head bowed. Her long platinum hair hung perfectly, without a strand out of place. Her poise and symmetrically chiseled features were almost enough to tempt him. She'd caught his lingering stare from time to time, and to her credit, she'd never exploited the opportunity. She was a patient hunter no matter what endeavor she partook in. Such was the way of the Xiiginns.

"Sion Shif reported in that the scout ship has just entered the Qegi star system," Kandra Rene said.

"Excellent. Now, if he uses the search protocols I gave him, he shouldn't have much trouble tracking Kladomaor."

Mar Arden stood up and noticed that Kandra Rene wouldn't meet his gaze.

"What is it?" he asked.

"This was a task that I could have carried out for you."

He caught the underlying edge to her tone. She had failed to use compulsion on their prisoner. Compulsion was one of the Xiiginns' most powerful tools, but if a species was able to resist, it could drive the Xiiginn involved to an unhealthy obsession.

They'd first come across this phenomenon with the Nershals. Like the Qegi, Mar Arden had found other ways to motivate the Nershals. The allure of technology just beyond their current capabilities had been a powerful motivator, but given an enemy to rally against, they'd quickly allied with the Xiiginns. The

Boxans often commented on the arrogance of Xiiginns, but what they'd failed to realize was that it was the Boxans' own arrogance that had set the species of the Confederation against them. Mar Arden had successfully used compulsion on many Boxans, and cycles ago he had set Kladomaor free in an attempt to gain access to the Boxan home world. No Boxan had been able to resist him the way Kladomaor had, but in the end it wasn't enough. They'd still wreaked havoc on Sethion.

"You want to pursue our lost Human prisoner?" Mar Arden said.

Kandra Rene looked up at him, and her dark violet eyes narrowed dangerously. "Yes," she said.

"You'll get your chance, but for now Sion Shif is on their immediate trail. Since he's successfully used his ability on one of the Humans, it was the best choice to send him with the scout ship," Mar Arden said.

Kandra Rene's hands had been clutched in front of her, and she released them to her sides, her rage tempered for a while at least.

"Why did they send us back to Nershal space?" Kandra Rene asked.

"We're hunting Humans, and this is the place they were first discovered. There must be a remnant gravity wave we can follow that was generated by the wormhole," Mar Arden said.

He enabled the large holoscreen and showed their position on the outskirts of the system. If the Nershals sent their own warships out here, they would have ample notice.

"Why did you bring us to the edge of the system?"

"What do you know about Boxan outposts, particularly their listening stations?" Mar Arden asked.

Kandra Rene circled around the holoscreen and looked at him. "They're used to collect data while observing primitive species. They're also the command and control center for the Star Shroud."

Mar Arden nodded. "Very good. They also have the ability to create wormholes, much in the way a Cherubian drive does."

"What purpose would that serve?"

"Can you think of nothing?"

Kandra Rene frowned in thought. "I could see them using this for communications, but did the Boxans use ships without Cherubian drives?"

"Yes, on both accounts. They used them for quickly sending data back to the Boxan home system, Sethion. They would also use small shuttlecraft to send their scientists to the listening stations. The scientists would perform their assigned tasks, check the systems and collect the recorded data, then bring them back to Command Central. Scientists would rotate in and out of the listening stations," Mar Arden said.

"I didn't know that," Kandra Rene said.

"Most Xiiginns don't. We kept it secret until the time of the great uprising."

"The Boxans had fail-safes ready to take down the listening stations wherever they were."

"Yes, but we suspect they left the Star Shroud networks intact. So if we could find one of these systems, we could decipher the shroud network and use that to map out all the species the Boxans had been studying," Mar Arden said.

Kandra Rene nodded and studied the holoscreen intently. "I don't know how you can pinpoint a former wormhole with any degree of accuracy. Confederation ships come in and out of here all the time."

"Now you're thinking like a starship commander. You're better than that."

Kandra Rene arched a brow, and her tail flicked to the side. "Show me entry points for all Confederation ships before the time of the Mardoxian priestess's capture."

The onboard AI updated the holoscreen, and Mar Arden smiled his approval.

Kandra Rene frowned. "We'll need to split the squadron to scan the system. I'm thinking it would be somewhere in the vicinity of the seventh planet in this system."

"Why?" he asked. He already knew the answer but wanted to know if she did.

"Because that's where the Boxan outpost in this system used to reside. So not the entire orbit. We should be able to narrow this down to a smaller area. A staggered approach from the squadron should help us find the anomalous wormhole remnant we're searching for," Kandra Rene said.

Mar Arden brought his hands together. "Excellent. I expect your presentation to Hoan Berend and his crew on the bridge to be equally impressive."

Kandra Rene's eyes widened. It was an honor for her to do this, and Mar Arden knew it. This would help alleviate her shame at failure to use compulsion on the Human for the time being, although he found her results puzzling. He'd seen Kandra Rene use compulsion on other species with skill. What was it about the Human physiology that made some of them resistant to compulsion? If Sion Shif performed as expected, they could figure out why they'd been in the Qegi star system to begin with.

Kandra Rene left him to bring Hoan Berend up to speed, and Mar Arden opened a secure channel to the scout ship. He had a couple of agents onboard the ship who would upload any data collected from the system, and he would then combine that with what they'd already collected. First, he would model the position of the Boxan space station in the Qegi star system.

"Now, what were you after?" Mar Arden muttered as he began his analysis. The answer was there, buried amid the details. His hunt had only just begun.

CHAPTER TWELVE

A couple of weeks had passed since Michael Hunsicker had convinced Chazen to consider building a life pod they could use to get back to Earth. Together, they'd gathered the materials they would need. They primarily worked in the main entryway that the crew of the Athena had used when they'd first come here, although that had been so long ago that he had trouble picturing it.

There was a lot to be salvaged from the listening station, but it wasn't an effort they charged into without some careful planning first. Chazen had made a list of materials available while Michael informed Mission Control of his intentions. At first there had been stunned silence, and after that wore off, Mission Control had offered to oversee their proposed plan. Michael was incredibly thankful for that, and it was good to know that his own species hadn't completely abandoned him.

Gary Hunter from Mission Control had told him there was initial resistance to using the Endurance for their close-proximity rescue mission. "You've got a friend in Edward Johnson," Gary said.

"What did he do?" Michael asked.

"There has been a lot of browbeating going on around here between government officials and the private corporate sector. Dux Corp must have some pretty good leverage because NASA agreed to have the Endurance come pick you up once you leave your cushy pad there on Pluto," Gary said.

Michael snorted as his thoughts returned to where he actually was. Sometimes while on these video calls he could almost believe that home was much closer than it really was.

"I know that look," Gary said. "We'll get you home, Michael. There are a lot of people working for this."

Michael clamped down on his emotions. The thought of getting home shattered his focus sometimes.

"I'm alright. Have there been any further comms from the Athena?" Michael asked.

"No, and nothing from the Boxan colony Kaylan talked about. Oh, here's a bit of news. There has been a new international proposal put forth to the United Nations today. They want to form an Earth Coalition Force, ECF, with a mandate to operate in space to defend the Earth."

Michael's eyebrows rose. "ECF? What would they be made up from?"

"That's the interesting thing. It's a mixed bag between elected leaders and representatives from the various militaries. While serving in the ECF, they would operate with authority only outside of Earth's atmosphere. Then, when their rotation is up, they'd have the option to return to their nation's military with full honors," Gary said.

Michael Hunsicker was a military man himself and, as such, knew that most militaries were steeped in traditions that didn't always meld with other nations' militaries. "It's an interesting concept. I think I read something years ago by a futurist of the time who talked about mankind's march toward a global society. If this ECF ever gets off the ground, this could be one of the first steps toward that."

"That's what a lot of people here at Mission Control think, but you know we're scientists and engineers," Gary replied.

"How did the other nations react to it?"

"Don't know yet. It was proposed today. The news media is doing what it does best, which is to get people scared so they'll keep watching the vids. My buddy, Kent, over in the IT department said there are already various groups forming on social media. While most people have accepted that there are aliens in our galaxy, there are still a lot of conspiracy nut jobs out there. The people in charge, though, that's a different story altogether," Gary said.

"I just hope they get their ducks in a row before it's too late," Michael said.

"History tells a different story. People won't start to believe the Xiiginns are coming until there are ships surrounding Earth. Even me saying it sounds strange, and I've been immersed in all this stuff since the beginning," Gary said, glancing over at another screen next to the camera. "Right, there was something else I'm supposed to ask you about. This life pod you're building —will it be able to accommodate Chazen as well?"

Michael frowned. "It could, but he says he won't leave."

"That is unfortunate. We have a proposal we'd like you to talk to him about."

INFINITY'S EDGE | 69

"Alright, what's the proposal?"

Michael spoke with Gary for almost another hour. Normally he'd not have taken so much time, but he needed to. When the call ended, Michael walked to the main entrance, where they'd been working on the life pod, and he found himself taking in his surroundings with the realization that his days here were numbered. At some point, the dark gray walls lined in a cyan light had become commonplace.

He rounded the corner and opened the large, metallic-gray doors. Chazen was hunched over one of the workbenches, focused on the internal components that would eventually go inside the pod.

There was nothing in the large open area that even closely resembled a pod. They'd built a large skeletal framework that basically looked like a twenty-foot-tall soccer ball. When they added each polygonal plate, it would reinforce the entire structure as a whole. There was no shortage of plating to be used for the outer hull. The material was the same as that used for the walls of the outpost. When finished, the life pod would look like a large, gunmetal-gray soccer ball traveling through space. The original design had been much smaller, but Michael had vehemently argued against that. He ostensibly made the argument that the extra room was needed because they weren't exactly sure how long Michael would be inside, but what he really hoped was that Chazen would consider climbing aboard and joining him on this journey.

He hastened over to Chazen's workbench, and the Boxan stopped what he was doing.

"You were gone longer than expected," Chazen said.

"Well, there was a lot to talk about," Michael said and proceeded to bring Chazen up to speed.

Chazen had very little to say and basically just acknowledged what Michael had told him.

"There is one more thing. We'd like to offer you asylum on Earth," Michael said.

Chazen frowned. "I'm afraid I don't understand."

"Come with me back to Earth," Michael said.

"My duty is here," Chazen replied.

"You've done your duty. You shouldn't stay here and die," Michael said.

Chazen tossed the tool he'd been holding onto the workbench and took a few steps away.

"I'm sorry," Michael said. "But if you stay here and the Xiiginn come here first, then . . ."

"I would destroy the outpost," Chazen said.

"And lose your life in the process. Come with me to Earth. Asylum grants you protection. We'll help you get back to the Boxans," Michael said and gestured toward the skeletal framework of the life pod. "All you have to do is climb aboard with me. The plan is for the Endurance to rendezvous with the pod and bring us to our lunar base. The message from the Athena said that the Boxans were coming as well. I'm sure there's a way to initiate the self-destruction of this place from Earth. There's no need for you to stay here," Michael said.

The Boxan's large ears twitched momentarily, disturbing his thick dark hair. Chazen closed his eyes and took slow, deep breaths. Michael had seen him do this before and knew it was a common practice of his culture.

Chazen's flaxen eyes opened, and he looked at Michael. "Very well. Tell your people I accept their gracious offer of asylum," he said.

Michael was stunned. He'd expected that Chazen would stubbornly choose to stay here. Michael had brought up the subject of Chazen returning to Earth with him months ago, and the Boxan had adamantly refused to even consider it. Perhaps it was building the life pod or the fact that Michael had been his only companion in over sixty years, and he realized he may have underestimated the desire not to be alone. And as beautiful as Pluto had turned out to be, it was nothing compared to stepping outside on a living, breathing planet. Michael believed that was what Chazen missed most of all, and if the Boxan hadn't agreed to come, he might have missed his last chance to do so.

They had a lot of work to do, and Michael was extremely happy that he would not be returning to Earth alone.

CHAPTER THIRTEEN

Over the next week, Chazen set a rigorous work schedule that Michael Hunsicker could hardly keep up with. Once the Boxan had made up his mind, he threw himself at the task. Despite the hard work and the hectic schedule that only allowed Michael to sleep four hours at a time, he found there was a spring to his step. The thought of going home invigorated him more than any stimulant could. And even though his rations had long since run out, Chazen had been able to get the food processors to spit out some sort of brownish gruel that had kept him alive. It tasted like runny eggs, with an extra emphasis on runny. Michael dutifully ate the concoction, knowing he needed to keep his strength up.

The life pod had transformed from an arrangement of chaotic components to that of a working pod virtually overnight, and Michael had gotten a quick update from Mission Control. The spaceship Endurance had successfully completed a short shakedown journey. Gary hadn't been too forthcoming with the details, but if they could hit their mark, the Endurance would have no issues finding them. In theory, the life pod could accommodate them for several weeks.

He'd been awestruck when they'd attached the outer plating of the life pod onto the framework. The Boxans had a device that changed the chemical state of the alloy used to create the walls of the outpost. Chazen had uploaded the design of the life pod into the device, and it broke down the metallic alloy sleeves into the preprogrammed shape. It looked as if someone had melted candlewax while it hung suspended in the air and worked it into a polygonal shape. Once the different sleeves joined together, there were no visible creases at all. There were also no windows. Once they were inside, their eyes and ears would be the small sensor array attached to the exterior of the hull. If they could have made engines, the pod would have flown. Unfortunately, designing complex ship engines was beyond their capability.

One of the biggest internal components of the life pod was the onboard computer that housed the Boxan's artificial intelligence, along with a record of all observations made during the station's lifecycle. Chazen considered it a small backup of all essential information in the event that they had to engage the self-destruct. They couldn't destroy the outpost when they left Pluto because they needed the power generator to create the micro-wormhole that would get them home. Neither of them was willing to accept the risk of a time-delay self-destruct because of the small possibility that something could go wrong.

Setting a course for the micro-wormhole required a precision that would severely tax the outpost's computer system. They could end up somewhere other than where they intended to be, or worse, which was something Michael didn't want to spend too much time thinking about. One thing they could count on was that space was so vast that there was little chance their micro-jump would take them to the surface of Mars, for instance. The gravest risk to them was the gravitational pull that could warp the wormhole, which would effectively slingshot them far away. This was an all-or-nothing effort to get Michael home and to give Chazen a chance to contact the Boxans.

"When would you want to engage the outpost's self-destruct?" Michael asked.

"Ideally, never. The outpost is also the command and control for the shroud network, which does provide a measure of protection to this star system," Chazen said.

"Would the Star Shroud be destroyed then?"

"Yes. The self-destruct protocols would spread to the shroud devices that reside in the Oort cloud," Chazen said.

A short while later they finished loading the pod. They'd had to move it outside so the phaze-emitter could be directed at the pod without risk to the outpost. There was little for Michael to do but watch Chazen use platforms that could support the weight of the pod. The Boxan then directed the platforms to move the pod a hundred meters from the outpost.

Michael wore his EVA suit from the Athena, which he hadn't worn since he'd left the spaceship, and putting it on felt like getting one step closer to home. He noticed that he had plenty of room inside it, which he attributed to living off rations and Boxan gruel. That thought led him to an image of Brenda Good-win, the Athena's medical officer, scolding him and going on about malnutrition. He'd been friends with Brenda since before the Athena mission. She had known Kathryn as well and had been at her funeral.

Michael walked out of the airlock onto the Plutonian surface. The sun looked like a lonely lantern in some far-off lighthouse, shining brightly in the distance. He couldn't keep the smile from his face. Each step he took brought him closer to home, and he had to keep himself from running headlong to the life pod. As he walked across Pluto's surface, memories of the Athena crew heading toward the Boxan outpost came to the forefront of his mind: Kaylan with her abilities; Zack Quick, who had initially deciphered the protocols used to access the shroud network; Dale Hicks and Katie Garcia, who were there to keep them safe; and even Jonah Redford, brilliant astrophysicist who foolishly attempted to take over the mission, leaving Michael shot and stranded. He'd been so focused on other things that he hadn't thought about Redford all that much. He wondered how they were all doing.

Although there was no structural reason to do so, years of habit from working in outer space caused Michael to duck his head as he entered the pod, where he took his position and waited for Chazen to join him. The Boxan stood outside and gazed back at the outpost that had been his home away from home for over sixty years. After a few moments, Chazen stepped aboard the pod, using his suit computer to close the hatch, and there was a slight gasp as the atmosphere pushed the vacuum away. The heaters inside had already warmed the small living space to minimal levels, and they could have taken their helmets off, but they were attempting something no one had ever tried before. If for some reason the hull was breached, their suits would be the only thing keeping them alive.

Chazen sat in his seat, and Michael brought up communications. They were still patched into comms from the outpost, so they had a live feed into Mission Control, where a duplicate countdown timer could be found. Michael whispered a prayer and engaged the countdown. Chazen opened the holo-interface from his suit computer. "The emitter has been brought into alignment."

The lighting inside the pod dimmed.

"Target locked," Chazen said.

Michael watched the countdown grind to zero.

"Engage."

Michael felt himself lift against the restraints of his seat. There was no antigravity in the pod.

"Matrix achieved. Commence jump," Chazen said.

Michael felt a crushing force press him back into his seat, and he cried out. Pinpoints of light pressed in on his vision as the interior of the pod pulled away from him. He felt as if he were launching on a rocket propelling him from Earth's atmosphere, and he was completely at its mercy. He squeezed his eyes shut, waiting for it to be over.

Michael Hunsicker found himself staring at the control panel in front of him. His eyes slowly focused on his surroundings.

"Commander, are you awake?" Chazen asked.

Michael blew out a breath as a wave of nausea swept over him. The nausea came from weightlessness, and he knew it would pass.

"Did it work?" Michael asked.

"Waiting for confirmation of our position."

Michael reached out to his own console, and after a few

moments an image appeared, showing them safely in the Goldilocks Zone of the solar system.

Eyes moist with unshed tears, Michael let loose a cry that ended with a laugh. They'd made it.

"Houston, this is Boxan Life Pod One. Do you copy?" Michael said.

There was no response. Michael waited a few moments and repeated himself.

"Boxan Life Pod One, we read you loud and clear. We have your position and are transmitting coordinates to the Endurance."

Michael's throat closed up with emotion. "We did it," he said to Chazen.

Chazen looked over at him, and for that moment at least, Michael saw something he hadn't seen in the Boxan's eyes before. Hope.

CHAPTER FOURTEEN

Main power had been restored to the Boxan stealth ship, and Kladomaor was heading to the bridge. The resonance chamber had been a good choice. He was better able to focus and would thus be able to perform his duties as battle commander with greater efficiency. After repairs had been made, the ship's computers had locked him out of the systems until he'd had the minimum required time in the resonance chamber. Boxan warship AIs were equipped to enforce certain protocols if there was sufficient evidence of risk to ship and crew. He'd ordered Gaarokk to override the AI, but the Boxan scientist had refused.

Ma'jasalax joined him on his way to the bridge. "You look more at peace," she said.

"Have you been able to locate the Athena?"

"No," Ma'jasalax said.

Kladomaor frowned. "You don't appear to be concerned."

"On the contrary, I'm quite concerned, but I don't think they perished."

Kladomaor entered the bridge, and the Boxan soldiers snapped a salute. He headed for the command couch, and Triflan stood at attention next to it.

"Situation report," Kladomaor said.

"We have main engines back online, but we've sustained heavy damage. We cannot go into stealth, and our combat capability is at thirty percent effectiveness," Triflan said.

Kladomaor engaged his neural implants and opened a connection to the ship's computer.

Gaarokk came over to them. "We've completed our analysis, and we think we were hit with some kind of pulse weapon that disabled most of the ship's systems."

Kladomaor glanced at the scientist and then over at his tactical officer. "The Xiiginns don't have the capability of firing their weapons while in a wormhole. Neither do we, for that matter."

"Correct, Battle Commander," Triflan said.

"So it can't be a weapon. There must be some other explanation," Kladomaor said.

"Perhaps this will help," Gaarokk said. The wall screen powered on. "I had the computer recreate our transit."

Kladomaor watched as the computer showed a mockup of the Boxan stealth ship and the small Human ship attached to them with the gravity tether. A wave of energy engulfed the Boxan ship, and he watched as the ship angled off and out of the wormhole.

Kladomaor frowned. "Slow the model down to twenty percent speed."

The computer model reset, and just before the pulse hit, their ship's gravity tether to the Athena had been disabled.

"Freeze it," Kladomaor said and looked at the others. "Why did they disable the tether?"

"We're not exactly sure," Gaarokk said.

Kladomaor looked at Ma'jasalax, who appeared to be waiting for him to get to her. "I know the Athena's design, and only Kaylan or Hicks would have been able to sever the tether from their bridge. I don't believe this is something Hicks would do on his own. The question is, why did Kaylan sever the tether in the first place?"

"I think severing the tether prevented the Athena from being destroyed," Gaarokk said. "Computer, replace model but follow the path of the Athena."

The computer model replayed, and it showed the pulse blast completely missing the Athena.

"They were still thrust from the wormhole as soon as the Cherubian drive went offline. What is the Athena's trajectory?" Kladomaor asked.

The computer showed multiple trajectories the Athena could have taken, along with the probability rates for each one. Now he knew why Ma'jasalax believed the crew of the Athena was alive.

"Kaylan must have sensed something was wrong and severed the gravity tether. It's the only explanation that makes any sense," Kladomaor said and moved his gaze back to Ma'jasalax.

"I didn't sense anything," Ma'jasalax said.

Gaarokk looked as if he were about to speak.

"What is it?" Kladomaor asked.

"We know the Mardoxian potential exists in Humans, but what if there's more? What if they could do more than even

Ma'jasalax can?" Gaarokk said, refusing to even look at Ma'jasalax.

"It's alright," she said. "Kaylan's abilities have been growing, but I think there's more to it than that."

Kladomaor's brows pushed forward in thought. "The Drar," he said.

Gaarokk and Triflan looked confused.

"That was my thinking," Ma'jasalax said.

"I don't understand," Gaarokk said.

"The signals we've been seeing that led us here are from the Drars. For some reason they wanted to meet the Humans without us but had surmised that the Humans couldn't make the trip on their own," Ma'jasalax said.

Kladomaor ground his teeth. "That's too many assumptions."

"Do you have a better explanation, Battle Commander?" Ma'jasalax asked.

"I'm not sure. The Drars were radically more advanced than us. We used their technology to make gains, but having the capability to detect ships using a Cherubian drive and then to disable one of them is a bit much to accept," Kladomaor said.

Triflan cleared his throat. "I've had my team analyze the data, and the energy reading of the pulse was just enough to take out our systems and nothing more."

Kladomaor glanced at the wall screen again. "So you're saying that if they'd wanted to destroy us, they could have. They simply wanted us out of the way for a while."

"Precisely," Triflan said.

"What do we do now?" Gaarokk asked.

"We go after them," Kladomaor said. "I won't abandon the crew of the Athena."

"Battle Commander," Triflan said, "I must advise caution. This was effectively a warning shot."

Kladomaor hardened his gaze. "We've been warned, but we're not going to stay away. I want to follow the trajectory for the highest probability rate of the Athena's path."

Triflan saluted him and returned to his station, and Ma'jasalax came to his side.

"We've been looking for evidence of the Drars since we saw their wars being fought in the great expanse," Ma'jasalax said, and her eyes grew distant in thought.

"You're wondering whether the Drars' message wasn't meant for us," Kladomaor said.

Ma'jasalax's eyes widened. "That's quite a leap for one not of the Mardoxian sect."

"Do you agree? Could the Drars have been waiting for a species like the Humans all along, and we were simply the courier vessel that brought them here?" Kladomaor asked.

"I don't think it's that simple," Ma'jasalax answered.

"No, it never is," Kladomaor said and took his place on the command couch, engaging the comms link throughout the ship. "Boxan crew, this is your battle commander. We're about to get underway. We're going after the Athena in order to fulfill our mandate to see the Humans safely returned to their star system. Battle Commander, out."

Kladomaor cut the link.

"Course ready, Battle Commander," Varek said from his navigation console.

"Make it so," Kladomaor said.

CHAPTER FIFTEEN

Sometimes Hicks got tired of being right. He'd been concerned that the Athena was too out of her depth for a journey like this, and he'd been right. Now they were stranded well away from any hospitable place. Sure, they could point the ship in a direction, and perhaps in a few hundred years they might actually make it to some destination, but none of them would be alive to see it. Maybe he should have pushed harder for them to return to Earth.

Hicks sighed. Fear and frustration were directing his thoughts, and it wasn't helping. He knew better than to be second-guessing every decision on any mission. He was better than that. They'd rolled the dice, taken a risk, and come up short. Plain and simple. They were still alive, so there was that at least. Plus, Kladomaor wouldn't have abandoned them.

"Was there something else you wanted to bring up?" Kaylan asked.

Hicks took a sip of his water and nodded. "Emma, would you tell Kaylan what you reported to me about Redford, please?"

The others on the bridge went silent, and Emma looked as if she'd rather be anywhere else than where she was right now.

"Jonah still has blackouts. We don't know why they occur and cannot predict when they will happen," Emma said.

"Yeah, but he's restrained, so what damage could he do?" Kaylan asked.

"When Brenda went to help you with Efren and Nikolai in Engineering, I was left alone with Jonah in the hydroponics lab. At some point, Jonah got up and went to the console," Emma said.

"Do you know if he did anything?" Hicks asked.

Emma shook her head. "It was blank by the time I got there."

"What do you think he did?" Kaylan asked Hicks.

"I'm worried that Redford sent a signal to the Xiiginns, letting them know we're right here," Hicks said.

"Now hold on a minute," Zack said. "He got to a console, but that doesn't mean he did anything."

"Athena," Hicks said. "Can you tell us what Redford was doing at the console in the hydroponics lab?"

"Apologies, Major, but I have no record of Dr. Redford accessing my systems from hydroponics. Furthermore, since the events at the Boxan space station, Dr. Redford's access to the computer system has been restricted," the AI said.

"There, you see?" Zack said.

Hicks smiled. "I'm surprised to find you so trusting. What if he covered his tracks somehow?"

Zack blanched, and Hicks watched as the hacker's thoughts

went into overdrive. He knew Zack could see patterns within patterns of data, and he was naturally suspicious of people. This made him great at investigations. "I hadn't considered it, but there would be logs of systems access."

"And Athena reports there was no access. Meaning no disrespect to the AI, but what if she's wrong?" Hicks asked.

"I'm not insulted by your query, Major," the AI said. "I can only report based on the information I have, and my records indicate that only mission specialist Emma Roberson accessed my system during this time."

Out of the corner of his eye, Hicks saw that Emma had brought her hand to her face, and he turned to look at her, but Emma was looking at Kaylan with crestfallen eyes.

"I'm so sorry. I left my console unlocked. I'm usually the only one in there, and with everything that's been going on . . ." Emma's voice trailed off.

Kaylan went over to Emma. "This isn't your fault. Athena, what did Jonah access using Emma's account?"

"Medical records for Zack, Commander."

Hicks glanced at Zack, who was just as dumbfounded as everyone else. "Which records?" Hicks asked.

"Brain scans, Major."

Hicks glanced at Zack. "Why would Jonah access your brain scans?"

Zack rubbed the back of his neck while he thought about it. "I don't know. I do make it a point to go see Jonah and try to talk to him. Sometimes he's lucid, and other times he mutters incoherently about the Xiiginns."

Kaylan frowned. "I didn't know you went to see Jonah."

Zack shrugged. "I never thought to mention it. I just started going to see him to make sure he was . . . He's part of the crew," Zack said firmly.

Hicks knew Redford was no one's favorite person on this mission. The man had a knack for rubbing people the wrong way. He'd even stretched Hunsicker's patience during their mission. Hicks looked at Brenda Goodwin, who was looking intently at her tablet computer.

Brenda looked up. "He was comparing Zack's brain scans to his own."

"Sounds like he was looking for a reason why the Xiiginns were able to use their compulsion on him and not Zack," Hicks said.

A stunned silence came over the Athena's crew, and Zack looked as if he almost felt guilty. Hicks knew that Redford had been sedated in the med bay and that there were times when, for no apparent reason at all, the astrophysicist showed volatile behavior. Brenda had said he was suffering from psychosis.

"If that's all he accessed, then we know he didn't cause our current predicament," Kaylan said.

"Agreed," Hicks replied.

"Commander," Emma said, "Brenda and I would like to run some additional tests on Zack to confirm a few things."

"Don't you think you should be asking me?" Zack asked.

Kaylan gave him a look.

"Alright, as long as it doesn't hurt, I'll be your guinea pig," Zack said.

Hicks chuckled. They still needed to figure out a way forward, but at least they could rule out Jonah Redford as a cause for the disaster.

CHAPTER SIXTEEN

Zack followed Emma and Brenda to the med bay after Kaylan dismissed them. In their time aboard the Athena, Zack hadn't even thought twice about Kaylan being the commander. She insisted that she was only 'acting commander' since the official mission still showed Michael Hunsicker as the Athena's commander. Zack didn't care about titles, and to him and the rest of the crew it seemed that Kaylan Farrow was their commander.

"How come you never told anyone about going to see Jonah?" Brenda asked.

"It never crossed my mind, really. I feel bad about what happened to him," Zack said.

"I would never have guessed that you were so compassionate," Emma said with a smile.

Zack let out a small laugh, feeling uncomfortable. "I know you guys have worked really hard on this, and we've had our share of surprises along the way, but do you think there's anything we can do for Jonah?"

"It's hard to say. We're still trying to understand exactly what was done to him," Brenda said.

They walked through the ship and made it to the med bay.

"According to his brain scans, it appears that certain parts of Jonah's brain have been irrevocably rewritten," Brenda said.

"So there's no chance to change everything back the way it was before?" Zack asked.

"We can't even do that back on Earth. I've been looking for ways to suppress the urges that come with the compulsion, but I haven't been successful," Brenda said.

Zack felt his mouth go dry. Kladomaor had insisted that there was nothing they could do for Jonah, but Zack had held out hope that they could prove the Boxan wrong. He'd spent more than a few moments during this voyage believing he'd been lucky to resist the Xiiginn's compulsion.

Brenda motioned for Zack to lie on the bed. Jonah was unconscious on a nearby bed. Zack didn't know what was worse —Jonah acting crazy or the fact that they had to sedate him to keep him from harming himself or others.

"How do you think the Xiiginn compulsion works?" Zack asked.

"Well, Gaarokk sent us quite a bit of information about that, and we also have our own observations," Brenda said.

Emma worked at one of the nearby consoles by his bed, and he was slowly laid flat.

"We think it works on a few different levels. First is the pheromones, where being in close physical proximity to the Xiiginns can cause behavioral changes in the beings around them.

We've seen similar things on Earth—from mammals to insects—but never something that could cross species like we see here. Even *we* emit pheromones," Brenda said.

"I guess that makes sense, but the Xiiginns have taken this to a whole new level," Zack said.

"Tilt your head back for me," Emma asked and then attached a small round disk to his neck.

Zack felt a slight pinch as the disk adhered to his skin.

"It's so we can get a clearer image of your brain. Do you remember when we had to do this in Houston?" Brenda asked.

Zack thought about it for a moment. The events bringing Zack onto the Athena mission had been a whirlwind tour of being poked and prodded. "I guess. They did so much to me before we left the ground that it all runs together."

Brenda chuckled.

"So pheromones give them access, but what about the rest? They made Jonah a sleeper agent, like they preprogrammed him to go off at a certain time," Zack said.

Emma nodded. "Let's not forget that we're dealing with a completely alien lifeform here. The Xiiginns might be humanoid with some extra appendages, but they're still alien and have evolved along a different evolutionary path."

"Appendages . . . nice. You know they can use their tails while they fight you? They lifted me up with it," Zack said.

Emma glanced at Brenda. Zack rarely talked about what had happened to him as a prisoner of the Xiiginns.

"I guess I never told anyone about that," Zack said sheepishly.

"No, you didn't," Brenda said. "But it can help you to talk

about these things. No matter what happened, we won't look at you any differently than we do, Zack."

Emma nodded and placed her hand on his shoulder. Zack was thankful for the support, but he didn't want to relive his captivity. Mostly, Zack just wanted to forget it. An image of Kandra Rene's violet-colored eyes flashed in his mind, causing him to shudder and shove those thoughts away.

"Okay, just relax now. None of this is going to hurt. We won't be sedating you for this because we need active brain scans," Brenda said.

Zack nodded. "Do you need me to think of something?"

Emma flipped her tablet computer around. "I'm going to show you some images and we'll map your reactions to them."

"Okay, go ahead," Zack said.

The first image to appear was Earth. Then it switched to a cup of coffee, and Zack smiled. He was a bit of a coffee nut, after all. The next image was of the Athena. The images progressed from different foods to various everyday objects and ultimately to pictures of the crew. Images of Kaylan came up more than once, and in one of them they were standing together on the tarmac about to board the space plane in Houston. The sun lit up the red highlights in Kaylan's hair, and Zack felt his lips curve upward as his chest became warm.

"I don't believe it," Emma said. "That's it!"

Brenda's mouth hung open, and she cycled through brain-scan images on the holoscreen nearest her. She then activated the holoprojector on the ceiling, and three-dimensional images of the brain were shown. Zack glanced at Emma, and she smiled down at him, unable to keep the excitement from her eyes.

"This series of brain images on the left are Jonah's, and these over here are yours from just now." The three-dimensional images of Zack's brain were green while Jonah's were amber-colored.

"I don't see anything," Zack said.

"This area here toward the middle is called the striatum. It's basically the reward system of the brain. This area of the brain is known to become active during attraction. When we showed you all those images, the ones of Kaylan sent fireworks through this part of the brain, similar to what we observe in Jonah," Brenda said.

Zack stared at the brain images and frowned. "I still don't get it."

Emma laughed. "Makes perfect sense. You are a man, after all."

Zack was still confused.

Emma rolled her eyes. "Love, Zack. Love is what you're seeing."

Zack raised his eyes to the highlighted brain images and then looked over at Jonah's, and understanding finally slammed into place.

"I bet that if we showed Emma pictures of her fiance back on Earth, we'd see something similar," Brenda said.

Zack swallowed hard. "So Jonah is in love with the Xiiginns?"

Brenda powered off the holoprojector, and the lights returned to normal. Zack sat up on the bed and swung his legs to the side.

"Something like that. It might be like becoming instantly addicted to a drug, but they're also able to implant complex messages," Brenda said.

Zack glanced over at Redford's unconscious form and sighed. "The reason for the aberrant behavior is because he's trying to resist, and it's killing him by slowly driving him insane."

Brenda gave him a serious look and nodded.

"Still doesn't explain why I wasn't vulnerable to the same thing," Zack said.

"Perhaps your feelings for Kaylan shielded you somehow," Emma said.

"Maybe," Zack said.

He wasn't sure what to think. He'd hoped they'd be able to reverse what had been done to Jonah, but he wasn't sure it was possible. Zack asked if he could leave, wanting to put some distance between himself and the med bay.

CHAPTER SEVENTEEN

K aylan was in the Athena's top observatory, trying to get a bead on where the Boxans could be. Sometimes she needed to get away from the bridge, and the top observatory had one of the best views on the entire ship. Radical advancements in silica glass development allowed for a large dome that provided an unfettered view of the stars. Kaylan retracted the ceramic alloy shield and saw the telescopic array off to one side. The array took pictures and enabled the AI to provide analyses of the images. She had an idea of where Earth was, but she couldn't tell which star was theirs in the star-filled sky. Even at best speed, they wouldn't make it home for thousands of years.

The door to the observatory opened, and Zack walked in. He smiled at her.

"You found my hiding spot," Zack said.

"Is this where you've been keeping yourself?" Kaylan asked.

"Sometimes. I retract the roof and try to convince myself that I'm looking up at the night sky in Chicago," Zack said.

Kaylan glanced above them. "I miss home, too."

They stood there watching the sky without saying anything at all. It was one of the rare moments of silence they both could enjoy.

"That's strange," Zack said and walked over to Jonah's standup workstation.

"What is it?" Kaylan asked, following him.

"Oh, it's one of the subroutines we had running to detect the Star Shroud devices. I thought Jonah disabled them when we first came to the Nershal star system, but I guess he left it running on a schedule to check periodically . . ." Zack's voice trailed off.

Kaylan nodded and saw Zack's gaze become more intense as he scanned the readout on the holoscreen.

"No, that can't be right," Zack said and glanced at her. "Our sensor array is detecting a signal similar to the Star Shroud."

Kaylan looked at the readout on the screen. She understood the concept when Zack explained it, but she couldn't make sense of the information on the holoscreen. Her eyes widened.

Zack nodded excitedly. "You see? This shouldn't be out here. The Boxans had no systems out here that I know of. I'll double-check with the AI, but I recall Gaarokk saying this was uncharted space for them as well."

"Can you pinpoint where the signal is coming from?" Kaylan asked.

"It'll take a little bit of time, but I should be able to." Zack stopped what he was saying and turned toward her. "This has to be intentional. This could be the Drars' way of hailing us or something."

Kaylan frowned. "Possibly. If it *is* something like the Star

Shroud, or an actual shroud, you might not be able to get directly to the source but only to the general vicinity."

"I should talk to Jonah," Zack said.

"I'm not sure that would be a good idea," Kaylan said.

"Why not?"

"I'm not sure there's a way we can help Jonah, and the longer this goes on, the more the man we knew slips away," Kaylan said.

Zack clamped his mouth shut. She knew he didn't like the thought of giving up, but Brenda's latest report showed more deterioration of Jonah's brain.

Zack swallowed and looked at the floor. "I knew things were getting worse for him, but I didn't . . . Jonah and I bumped heads a lot, but he didn't deserve this."

Kaylan put her hand on his shoulder and gave him a gentle squeeze. "I know," she said softly.

Zack glanced at the holoscreen. "The signal is getting weaker."

"We might be moving away from it," Kaylan said.

Zack adjusted the sensor array, and the signal returned.

Kaylan headed for the door. "Send those coordinates to the bridge. I'll begin running numbers to see how far away it is."

Zack said he would, and she left for the bridge.

CHAPTER EIGHTEEN

I t took some convincing, but Zack eventually got Brenda to allow him to bring Redford to his lab in the top observatory. Hicks and Katie were with him just in case they had to restrain Jonah. There were times when Redford seemed quite distant from them—like he was standing there, but the lights weren't on inside his mind.

"Let's give him a little bit of space," Zack said.

Hicks and Brenda backed away. Redford closed his eyes and began nodding.

"I must make contact— No!" Redford said.

Jonah Redford had already been a thin man, but now he was so skinny that his facial features looked severe, and six weeks of beard growth made the astrophysicist look feral. Brenda had told Zack that Jonah was reluctant to eat.

Redford spun around, seeming to notice where he was for the first time. His eyes darted to Zack, and it took him a few moments to recognize him.

"You're alright, Jonah. We're on the Athena. This is your lab. Do you remember?" Zack asked.

Redford's brows pushed forward, and then he glanced toward the holoscreen that showed a digital dashboard of his ongoing research.

"I kept your research going for you as best I could," Zack said.

Redford stepped toward the console below the holoscreen, and Zack noticed Hicks purposefully place his hand on the stunner he carried.

"No, no, no," Redford said.

Zack came to his side and used his implants to change the data on the holoscreen. "I need you to take a look at this. We started getting a response to the Star Shroud protocols you and I set up."

Redford's eyes narrowed as he focused on the screen. "No, no, that can't be right," Jonah said, and his face crumpled in pain. "Contact. Must make contact— NO!"

Redford extended his hands, and his gaze widened at the severe scar tissue all over his forearms and hands—the result of the harsh burns he'd received when he'd signaled the Xiiginns their location.

Redford squeezed his eyes shut and brought his hands to his head.

"The Xiiginns can't find us here. They don't know where we are," Zack said.

Redford looked at him with relief. "I tried to stop myself, but I just couldn't."

Zack nodded. "I know you did. We need your help now. You set up an automatic protocol to seek out new Star Shroud devices, and we got a response."

"A response?" Redford said. "Where?"

Zack pulled up the coordinates Kaylan had been able to piece together for them, and Redford kept his hands clenched as he peered at the information on the screen.

"Need a better look," Redford muttered. He went over to the console and began inputting commands.

Hicks took a step closer, and Zack waved him off.

The sensor array outside the observatory shifted position, and new data feeds showed on the holoscreen.

Redford started to enter more commands, then stepped back. "No, I can't," he said and winced. "Must keep . . . it out."

Redford collapsed onto the floor, crying out.

"We don't have long," Brenda said.

Zack nodded and squatted down in front of Redford. "You moved the sensor array. What are you looking for?"

"Shroud network," Redford said. "But it's not safe." Redford shuddered and began rocking in place. "Too much radiation . . . the poles."

Redford's eyes fluttered and his whole body went into convulsions.

Brenda ran over. "He's having a stroke," she said.

They eased Redford over and laid his head on Brenda's lap.

"Isn't there anything you can do?" Zack asked.

Brenda shook her head. "We have to wait for it to pass," she said.

Hicks glanced over at Zack. "Did you get what you needed?" he asked.

Zack couldn't tear his eyes away from Jonah.

"Look at me," Hicks said and tipped Zack's face up.

"There's got to be something we can do for him," Zack said.

Redford stopped convulsing, and he seemed to pass out.

Zack's mouth went dry. That could have been him lying on the floor. Though it had been weeks, Jonah was still fighting the Xiiginns' influence, and the fight was going to kill him. Zack clenched his teeth and surged to his feet. Molten fury gathered inside him. He hated the Xiiginns with everything he had. He kicked the chair across the room, and it crashed into the wall as he balled his hands into fists. His breath came in gasps.

Hicks came over to him. "You need to calm down. I don't like what they've done to him any more than you do."

Zack jerked away from Hicks. "I want to hurt them," he said and heard the crack in his voice. "Kandra Rene, Sion Shif, Mar Arden, and all the rest of them."

His heart felt as if it would pound right out of his chest, and the walls were closing in on him. Katie came over and whispered something to Hicks. Hicks left them and helped Brenda get Redford back to the med bay.

Zack glanced at her with tears blurring his vision.

"Don't tell me to calm down," Zack said.

Katie held her hands up in front of her chest. "I wasn't going to."

"Almost every night, I lie down with Kaylan, but when I close my eyes it feels like I'm back in that pit," Zack said.

"I know," Katie said.

Zack frowned. "How do you know?"

"Because Kaylan told me about the nightmares. You were a prisoner. They hurt you. They hurt Jonah."

Zack sighed heavily. "He's going to die, isn't he?"

Katie gave him a sympathetic look and nodded.

Zack's throat thickened. "I didn't even like him. He always acted so superior to everyone else, but . . ."

"We're all in this together. We're on the same crew," Katie said.

They didn't speak for a few moments while Zack just stared at the overturned chair he'd kicked.

"You know, in the pit with all the mutants fighting, I didn't want to hurt anyone. Etanu was so angered by some of the things I did or wouldn't do. He's a soldier, and he sees only one way to deal with threats, but with the Xiiginns I want to be more like him. I hate them so much," Zack hissed.

Katie placed her hand on his back and rubbed it soothingly. Zack blew out a breath, and all the pent-up anger seemed to drain away from him.

"Thanks," Zack said.

"I'm your friend."

"I know," he said and frowned. "Is there something wrong with me for saying all that stuff?" Zack asked.

Katie shook her head. "No, there is something right about it. It means that you're coming to grips with what's happened to you. Hating the Xiiginns who hurt you isn't wrong."

Zack walked over and picked up the overturned chair. "I didn't want to say all that stuff to Kaylan. She's got enough to deal with."

"That's where you're wrong. Kaylan is there for you. She'll understand," Katie said and walked over to the holoscreen. "Now, what does this stuff mean?"

Zack glanced at the screen. "Jonah mentioned radiation. Athena, what do these new readings mean?"

"Preliminary analysis suggests that there is a powerful

magnetic field near where the shroud signal is coming from," the AI said.

"Can the ship make it through it?" Zack asked.

"The ship would sustain some damage, but all organics onboard would die from radiation exposure," the AI said.

"Great," Zack said.

"If we had the instrumentation on the Boxan stealth ship, there might be a path through the field, but that is beyond our current capabilities," the AI said.

"Well, that's that," Katie said.

Zack frowned in thought. "Not necessarily," he said.

"You heard the AI," Katie said.

"I did, but the AI can't account for all our resources."

"Resources?"

Zack smiled. "Kaylan," he said.

Together he and Katie headed for the door. Zack didn't think that whoever sent the signal would bring them here just to die on the approach, which meant there had to be a way to get through.

CHAPTER NINETEEN

K aylan sat alone in the Athena's mess hall. She'd just finished her breakfast, and she took a sip of coffee that Zack often referred to as a cup of ambition. Efren and Nikolai had been there earlier, both joking about where to find the best fishing. Efren preferred deep sea fishing in the Atlantic while Nikolai preferred fishing in rivers and lakes. Kaylan didn't have an opinion, but she had enjoyed the playful banter. When they left, she'd decided to take advantage of a few moments alone to sit and enjoy the silence. She disconnected her neural implants to the Athena's computer systems and just sat perfectly still.

Ma'jasalax had been teaching her about meditation and how its practice was one of the pillars of Boxan society. The Boxan approach to a meditative state was similar to what Kaylan had read about elsewhere. There were different ways to achieve a meditative state, and it wasn't just sitting still in a quiet room, but that was one of them. Ma'jasalax had often taken her to the resonance chamber aboard the Boxan ship. The resonance chamber was a large, peaceful garden—maintained by each of Kladomaor's crew—where they played recorded sounds from the forests of the Boxan home world. She couldn't imagine NASA ever devoting so much space to an onboard retreat on future spaceships, but most of the Athena crew liked to do a rotation through Emma's hydroponic garden, so perhaps the idea had merit.

"Kaylan, please report to the bridge," Hicks's voice said over the ship's comms.

Kaylan used her neural implants to reconnect to the Athena's computer systems. She acknowledged the message and a few minutes later was back on the bridge. Zack was working on a smaller holoscreen at the conference table. They were all there except for Efren and Nikolai, who were working in Engineering, and Brenda and Redford, who were in the med bay.

"Zack, are you ready?" Hicks asked.

Zack gave him a half nod while performing some last-minute tasks on his screen and then activated the main display. A blinking dot marked the Athena as the only thing in the vicinity.

"With Jonah's help, we estimated the approximate origin of the shroud network signal response. But there doesn't appear to be anything there," Zack said.

"If it *is* a Star Shroud, we should be able to see past it," Kaylan said.

"That's how it worked back home, but Gaarokk said the tech used for the Star Shrouds was based on Drar technology the Boxans found," Zack said.

Kaylan studied the information onscreen. Several smaller

windows had the sensor array output, and she took a moment to absorb the results.

"Redford looked at this and was saying something about too much radiation," Zack said.

Kaylan frowned in thought. "That's because whatever is there is surrounded by a powerful magnetic sphere. Hmm, that's strange. Were you able to map the actual shroud devices?"

"I tried, but we're just getting the initial signal. All my attempts at anything more have failed," Zack said.

"Commander, I have a theory," the AI said.

"Go ahead, Athena," Kaylan said.

"There is a substantial probability that the signal is for us specifically. My analysis of the sensor data shows that the signal only started broadcasting in our direction after we arrived," the AI said.

"How could you possibly know if the signal was sent before we got here?" Hicks asked.

"The commander ordered that we make a sweep with the sensor array of the area to determine where we are. When Zack found the signal from Dr. Redford's equipment, I correlated the data with what I already had and then calculated the probability to—"

"Athena," Zack said with a smile. "I think Hicks was just looking for a high-level explanation and not the actual formulas you used to form your theory."

"Oh," the AI responded. "In essence, the signal used is short-ranged and only broadcasting in our direction. The analysis shows that the signal loses much of its integrity the farther away it goes."

"So you're saying the signal is being intentionally sent to us?" Hicks said.

"Precisely, Major."

Hicks glanced at Kaylan. "I don't like this. Too many unknowns."

"What do you suggest?" Kaylan asked.

"That we continue to try to find Kladomaor."

"Anyone else?" Kaylan asked and glanced at the others.

Zack looked back at her. "Wouldn't Kladomaor have found us already if he could?"

"Their ship could have taken damage like us, but once they get underway, the Boxans will come looking for us," Hicks said.

Kaylan glanced around at all of them. They'd been trained to one degree or another to focus on the problems they could deal with. "We have no way of knowing where Kladomaor is or . . . if their ship was destroyed, and we don't have the resources to wait here forever. Star Shrouds were used around star systems that hosted planets with life. Perhaps the Drars used them for something similar." Kaylan pulled up a plot for best speed to the anomaly. "We could be there in a few days, and perhaps we'll learn more along the way."

"There is no way we can know the intentions of whatever is sending that signal," Hicks said.

"Well, they want our attention, so that says something," Zack said.

"That's the bait. I want to know if there's a hook inside," Hicks said.

Kaylan pressed her lips together in thought.

"What if we get ourselves into a situation we can't get out of?" Hicks asked.

"Like being stranded light years from home?" Zack asked with half a grin.

Hicks smiled. "Something like that."

"We could wait here and see if Kladomaor finds us," Kaylan said. "In the meantime, that signal will still be there, but there's no guarantee that nothing else will change. As we're all well aware, this ship isn't designed for the challenges of deep space. So the longer we stay where we are, the more we run the risk of something else going wrong—stress fractures on the hull and broken equipment. The list goes on and on. Right now we have the capacity to investigate this signal that was sent to us. I, for one, don't believe it was by accident. Perhaps we were brought here. We were chasing after the Drar, who were even more advanced than the Boxans. What's to say they didn't orchestrate the events that put us just days away from that shroud signal?"

Several crewmembers nodded their heads, accompanied by worried looks from others around the conference table.

"Now, if the Drars could do all those things, do you honestly think that if they wanted to come out here and get us, we could get away? I believe the signal is an invitation of some sort, and I'd much rather cautiously approach, gathering data along the way"— she glanced at Hicks—"and having you think of all those 'what-if' scenarios so we can put together contingency plans for what we can and acknowledge what we can't do anything about."

She still saw the underlying fear in the eyes of those around her. She felt it herself, but she also saw a determination that focused their minds on identifying problems. Michael Hunsicker had often said that identifying and solving one problem at a time was the best way to survive any mission in space. Solve enough problems and you get to live another moment and hopefully get to return home.

"We have a way forward," Kaylan said. "We're going to the shroud."

Zack cleared his throat. "What about the high levels of radiation? One of the last things Redford said was something about the poles."

"We'll need to study the magnetosphere and determine where the poles are. We might be able to find a safe approach that way," Kaylan said.

They spoke for a few more minutes and assigned different tasks, then she dismissed them and they went to work.

"You've changed," Hicks said.

"What do you mean?" Kaylan said.

"Ever since we lost Michael I've occasionally wondered how things would have gone if he'd been in charge," Hicks said.

Kaylan gave a small laugh. "I ask myself that all the time."

"Yeah, but lately I don't wonder so much anymore, and I think after today not ever again," Hicks said. "I'm trained to assess risks and think of ways of overcoming whatever obstacles come in our path."

"I know. That's why I rely on you so much. Together, we make a good crew. We balance each other out."

Hicks smiled. "Yeah, but you do the same thing and on a level much higher than anyone I've ever met before. Katie and I have served under all different types of commanders during our career. In special cases, there are those who are just plain brilliant. Those are the ones to stick close to."

Hicks left, and Zack came over. "I'll follow you anywhere, Commander," Zack said, imitating Hicks's Southern accent.

Kaylan punched him in the arm. "You're such an idiot."

Zack smiled. "I know, but he's right."

Kaylan smiled. She was glad they all believed in her. It really meant a lot. She just hoped their faith wasn't misplaced. She had no idea what the intentions of whoever sent that signal were, but they couldn't just wait out here in the middle of nowhere to find out.

CHAPTER TWENTY

Michael and Chazen were still in the life pod, but the Endurance had come along and scooped them up, and they were on their way to Armstrong Lunar Base. From there, they both would go to Earth after decontamination protocols were performed. When Michael had left Earth on the Athena, the Endurance had still been two years from scheduled completion.

There were no windows on the life pod, but the sensors were able to build a picture of the Athena's sister ship. The size and shape were reminiscent of the Athena, with the half-saucer-shaped front and rear engines, but that was it. Michael frowned at the image, looking at all the added things attached to the hull. Chazen had spotted it first, but it took Michael some time to realize that the spaceship Endurance had been weaponized. Michael couldn't begin to guess what weapon systems had been forced onto the Endurance, but he knew there had been a lot of engineering involved to get them in place. Humanity had been putting weapons in space for eighty years—some were hidden in satellite systems, ready to take out other nations' satellites or a target on Earth—so the concept of weapons in space wasn't exactly a new concept, but putting them on a spaceship designed for scientific exploration was. Michael had been in the military, and he knew that the Endurance wasn't a warship, but it was the only thing they had at the moment. Michael guessed that at least some people were taking the Xiiginn threat seriously.

A U.S. Air Force Colonel by the name of Kyle Matthews commanded the Endurance. Like the Athena, the Endurance's crew was a mix of astronauts and military personnel but with more of the latter for the Endurance. Michael knew the original plan had been for the Endurance to go to Pluto for Michael and Chazen; however, with the radical changes to the spaceship, and since it was a short trip, they would stay aboard the life pod until they reached the lunar base.

Since they'd come into contact with the Endurance and were almost to the lunar base, Michael could hardly sit still. The life pod was becoming cramped. Chazen seemed to take this in stride, and Michael tried to contain his excitement, but he was happy to finally get home.

"Commander," Kyle Matthew's voice said over comms.

"Go ahead," Michael said.

"I thought you'd like to know that we're inserting into a lunar synchronous orbit. After that, we'll detach the pod and you'll be shuttled to the base," Kyle said.

"Sounds good. We appreciate you coming to give us a ride," Michael said.

"Glad we could help," Kyle said.

The Endurance slowed its speed and eventually came to the

position that made shuttle approach to the lunar base feasible. The life pod had nothing in the way of gravity fields or inertia dampeners, but the Endurance's gravity field was able to extend to the life pod for short durations. This meant that Michael and Chazen had to stand on the walls for a while. Once they were in position, the gravity field was withdrawn. During the planning phase, Michael had thought they would exit the pod and shuttle down to the lunar surface, but Chazen insisted that they needed the equipment they'd brought with them and that the pod must remain intact.

They detached from the Endurance, and Michael didn't even hear the clamps release. It was a bit unnerving to have no windows at all. Michael could see what was going on with the small holoscreen, but it wasn't the same. The holoscreen showed the shuttle moving into position below them while the Endurance moved away from them. Chazen worked on the holo-interface. The Boxan had a device that would allow them to stay with the shuttle without physically attaching to it. Chazen had described it as a micro-field generator that allowed them to hover along the shuttle's surface. It was extremely power-intensive, which was why they hadn't been able to use it for the few days it had taken the Endurance to bring them here. Chazen engaged the device and gave Michael a nod.

"We're ready," Michael said.

"Copy that. We'll take you forward nice and easy," Kyle replied.

Michael felt his body press against the straps as the shuttle started to move. His eyes were locked onto the screen. The lunar base was comprised of a few surface buildings, with the bulk of the base located underground. One thing NASA had learned was that digging out caverns on the moon was relatively easy to do. The challenge had been getting the equipment in place.

The shuttle approached the designated landing area for them and set the pod down. Lunar base personnel came over with tethers. Chazen had assured them that they could literally pull them down to the lunar surface, and he'd been right. They cleared the shuttle, and Chazen disengaged the device. The moon's gravity did the rest. They already had their full spacesuits on, and Michael expended the atmosphere. Chazen motioned for him to open the door, and Michael couldn't keep the eager smile from his face. He opened the door and saw five lunar-base personnel in their EVA suits, waving at him. They were the first people he'd seen in person in about six months, and he had to fight to keep his eyes from misting up.

"Commander Hunsicker, welcome to lunar base. My name is Alissa Archer."

Michael smiled widely and knew he must look like a fool, but he didn't care. Alissa and the others smiled and waved. He stepped out of the pod and waited for Chazen. The Boxan's stooped form exited the life pod, and he unfolded to his full ten-foot stature. Alissa and the others' mouths were agape in wonder.

"On behalf of all humanity, I'm very pleased to welcome you to lunar base," Alissa said to the Boxan.

Chazen glanced down at her. Michael noticed that the Boxan had kept his helmet clear so they could see his face.

"Thank you," Chazen said.

"If you both will follow me, we'll guide you to decontamination chambers set aside for you. The rest of the crew here will move the pod to the adjacent chambers so you will have access to your things," Alissa said.

Michael was glad for that. He knew there would be plenty of people chomping at the bit for access to alien technology.

Chazen glanced at Michael and then back at Alissa. "I appreciate that . . . Are you the commander of this station?"

"I am," Alissa said.

"In that case, thank you, Commander," Chazen said.

They followed Alissa to the surface capsule they'd use to reach the base's interior. Inside was an elevator that would take them below the surface. They rode the elevator down, and Alissa led them to their temporary housing. They passed very few people, but anyone they did come upon looked at Chazen in awe.

The Boxan glanced at him.

"Well, you are quite tall," Michael said.

Chazen didn't reply.

"Hold on one moment, please," Alissa said and accessed her suit's computer. "Change of plans. I'm to take you to a comms station immediately."

Michael frowned. "Is there a problem?"

Alissa frowned. "I'm not sure, but they want to speak to both of you immediately."

"What about decontamination protocols?" Michael asked.

"We'll do what we can to minimize exposure, but this sounded urgent," Alissa said.

She led them through a series of short corridors to a small command center, stopping outside the door and removing her helmet. "I don't believe you're contaminated with anything that's going to harm us; otherwise, Michael would have been affected long before now. So if you want to remove your helmet, you can do so on my authority."

They'd already gone through a basic decon room before even

coming inside the base. Michael removed his helmet, and Chazen retracted his into his suit. Alissa seemed surprised by this for a moment, and Michael thought that this was how he must have looked when he'd first met Chazen. She opened the door, and the people inside turned around at the sound of Chazen's heavy footfalls.

"Change in plans, people," Alissa said, snapping them out of their reactions at seeing their first alien.

Michael had been watching Chazen's reactions and was quite pleased with how the Boxan was coping so far.

"Commander," Michael said, and Alissa leaned over to him. "If all nonessential personnel could give us a few minutes here, I think that would be good."

Alissa nodded. "All nonessentials, clear the room," she ordered.

Several people left for the opposite exit and the rest returned to their stations. More than one person kept glancing over at them, and Michael could hardly blame them.

"Commander," a younger man said, "I have Houston on comms."

"Put them on screen, Jack."

The main wall screen came on, and Michael saw Edward Johnson's face appear, along with Gary Hunter.

"Welcome back, Michael," Ed said.

"Thank you," Michael replied.

Ed turned his gaze to Chazen. "There are a lot of people anxious to meet you. I wish I had more time to give this occasion the attention it deserves, but we find ourselves in need of your expertise," Ed said, and his gaze included Michael.

"What do you need?" Michael asked.

"Our gravity-wave detectors reveal an anomaly on the fringes of the interior solar system."

"By Pluto?" Michael asked.

Ed shook his head. "No, far from its orbital path. We'd like you to take a look at the sensor data and see if you can tell us what this is."

Michael glanced up at Chazen, and the Boxan considered the request.

"I'll look at the data," Chazen said and glanced down at Alissa. "I'll need access to my equipment sooner than expected."

"Equipment?" Ed asked.

"We salvaged what we could bring from the station, including the AI," Michael said. "I'm guessing we're going to need it."

Chazen nodded. "It will help speed up the analysis."

Alissa was about to speak, but Edward Johnson cut her off.

"Commander, give them whatever they need. Time is of the essence, and until the ECF is formally ratified, we need to move forward," Ed said.

"I understand the need to move forward, but you don't have the authority to approve this," Alissa said.

"You're right I don't, and you'd be fully within your rights to deny the request, but what if Chazen can identify whether the Xiiginns have found our solar system? The sooner we learn that, the better we'll be able to prepare."

Michael watched as Alissa considered what Ed said and then gave a nod. "They'll have what they need to identify the anomaly."

Michael got the sense that Alissa was a stickler for the rules. Most people who worked in space did so because they were saving lives. There were no space cowboys. But sometimes, in the face of the unknown, some of the red tape had to be cut through quickly. Chances were that if Alissa waited for the proper authority to grant the request, they would do so anyway.

"Alright, let's get to work," Alissa said.

So much for a long rest isolated in a decontamination chamber, but Michael didn't care. He was happy to be among his own kind, and he felt a renewed sense of determination to help Chazen get back to his home, no matter how long it took.

CHAPTER TWENTY-ONE

The young Xiiginn stared smugly in the video log message that Mar Arden had just paused. Sion Shif had tracked multiple wormholes from the Qegi star system, and analysis had revealed that the Boxans had been keenly interested in one of the moons in the system. When the attack had been ordered, the Boxans destroyed the site they'd been working on. Mar Arden knew about an ancient species called the Drars that the Boxans highly revered, and somehow Mar Arden couldn't convince himself that the Boxans return to the Qegi star system had been purely academic. He glanced at Sion Shif's face onscreen and continued the message.

"We've discovered a wormhole remnant that appeared to have been opened from inside the asteroid base. The destruction of the base must have covered up any residual distortions. By the time you receive this message, we will have gone through to follow," Sion Shif said.

Mar Arden felt his tail flick in response to his rising anger, but he got himself under control and gave himself a sharp mental shake at such a blatant display of emotion. Only Kladomaor would open up a wormhole inside an asteroid space station to escape its destruction. He wanted to hunt them down, and now it looked like he wouldn't get the chance.

Hoan Berend sent him a message summoning him to the bridge, so Mar Arden scowled at the image of Sion Shif's face and closed the video. He knew he should be proud of his young operative, but he also knew the commander of the scout ship would blunder along, believing he could catch a battle commander like Kladomaor unaware; however, the events that had taken place in the Nershal star system spoke volumes about what the old battle commander was willing to do to keep the Humans out of Xiiginn hands.

Mar Arden headed for the bridge. Kandra Rene waited outside for him.

"More ships have been reporting in," Kandra Rene said.

"Do you know what they want?" Mar Arden asked.

Kandra Rene shook her head, and they entered the bridge. Mar Arden went in first, as was his right, and headed directly over to Hoan Berend.

The commander sat in his chair and glanced up at Mar Arden's approach. A haughty smile played across his face, and Mar Arden began to consider whether to have the ship commander killed.

"You've summoned me," Mar Arden said.

Hoan Berend shook his head and gestured toward the main holoscreen. The face of an older Xiiginn filled the screen, and his dangerous gaze peered down at Mar Arden.

Mar Arden instantly bowed his head. Those on the bridge stopped what they were doing and stood up to salute the supreme leader.

"Garm Antis," Mar Arden said. "I had no idea you'd be coming and with an entire strike legion."

That was a lie, of course, and someone like Garm Antis would be able to see right through it, but this was how the game was played.

"Have you located the home of this Human species?" Garm Antis asked.

Mar Arden knew he couldn't stall any longer. Sion Shif and the scout ship had left the Qegi star system more than two cycles ago, and he'd been stalling his efforts until he received the update. The timing of Garm Antis's appearance with a strike legion of warships seemed almost too timely for it to be happenstance.

"Only just so. Some would say your timing is fortuitous," Mar Arden said and took control of the main holodisplay's output. "We tracked this wormhole to a singular star system with nine planetary bodies."

Garm Antis glanced at the data feed and narrowed his gaze. "That's not a traditional wormhole signature coming from a Cherubian drive."

"The Human vessel appears not to have a Cherubian drive. I suspect that the Boxan monitoring station in the Human star system is completely intact, including the Star Shroud devices," Mar Arden said.

Garm Antis glanced back at him, and his platinum-colored hair gracefully followed his movements. "You've done well, Mar Arden," he said and glanced past him, focusing on Hoan Berend.

"Attach your ship to the strike legion. You'll be joining us when we leave."

"I've given you what you asked for, and I'd like permission to take a ship and pursue the Boxan/Human team that escaped our attack," Mar Arden said. No sooner had the words escaped his lips than he wanted to take them back.

Garm Antis regarded him for a moment. "You've done well, but you presume much. Hoan Berend has informed me that the ones you're so eager to find are already being pursued. Besides, I need your talents for this new species," he said.

Mar Arden bowed his head. "I would advise caution. We may not be unopposed there."

"The Humans can hardly resist us," Garm Antis said.

"I meant the Boxans," Mar Arden said.

The supreme leader glanced at the ship commander as if he needed to check whether or not what Mar Arden had just said was reliable. Failure exacted a toll, and he had to keep the wounding of his pride to a minimum.

"What evidence do you have to support this?" Garm Antis asked.

"I have no hard evidence, but based on the Boxans' actions in the Nershal star system and the lengths they went through to keep the Humans from falling into our hands, it seems highly likely. The Boxans risked open conflict in another species' star system, and that species was not formally aligned with them. As you're aware, they escaped their asteroid base, but they went in a direction away from charted space. All these things are highly irregular for the Boxans," Mar Arden said.

A Xiiginn came up to Garm Antis and leaned in to say something only the supreme leader could hear. Garm Antis looked back at Mar Arden. "There is conjecture, and then there is skilled analysis. The Boxans don't wield power among the stars as they once did, and they haven't won a battle against us in some time. The Confederation believes they're broken, and we're observing the final death throes of those who once believed they were our superiors."

"Perhaps," Mar Arden said, neither agreeing with the supreme leader nor disagreeing with him.

"Once our forces are ready, we will go to this new star system and finally gain access to a working Star Shroud network, not to mention a new species to rule," Garm Antis said.

The primary display went back to normal as communications from the supreme leader's flagship was cut. It wasn't often that Mar Arden was dismissed, and it seemed that his tolerance for it declined the higher in rank he rose. He glanced at Hoan Berend, but the Xiiginn's gaze was fixed on his console.

"What is it?" Mar Arden asked, trying to keep the ire from his tone.

"We're receiving orders," Hoan Berend said.

Mar Arden waited for the commander to continue, and with each passing moment had to keep from lashing out at him.

"It seems that Garm Antis has grown tired of waiting. We leave for the Human star system now," Hoan Berend said.

Mar Arden felt a thrill of energy spike through him.

Kandra Rene leaned over to him. "I felt that," she said in a low voice.

Mar Arden glanced at her but didn't say anything. It appeared that he was to be part of the subjugation of another species, and the thought of it appealed to the primal hunger that resided in all Xiiginns—the hunger that drove them to hunt and rise to become the dominant force in the galaxy.

CHAPTER TWENTY-TWO

Kaylan made the crew of the Athena snag sleep shifts in a rotation, which included herself. The closer they got to their destination, the harder it was to sleep. No one was getting any rest, and they were all on edge. She hadn't felt anything like this since they'd first gone to Pluto.

She closed her eyes and tried to peer ahead with her senses. Like all the other times, she felt as if she were coming up against something slippery that wouldn't allow her to focus, but she didn't let that perturb her efforts. She knew so much more now, and she pressed onward, trying different things. Their sensors confirmed that this Star Shroud was more of a planetary shroud and that there was no star in this area. The AI theorized that there hadn't been a star in this area for millions of years—hardly the blink of an eye when dealing with the universe—but believing that they were approaching something that could be millions of years old left quite the impression on all of them.

The shroud was spherical in shape. Kaylan continued to

probe with her senses, delving further beyond where the shroud should have ended, and each time she experienced some success she was shut out again. She caught glimpses of some type of structure inside but not enough to accurately describe what it looked like. Something was inside, and it knew they were coming. The fact that it could also detect Kaylan's attempts to see inside was both surprising and unsettling. Hicks hadn't liked that fact one bit. She recalled a time when she hadn't wanted anyone to know about her remote viewing capability, but they'd come to rely on it, and it hardly occurred to her to hide anything from them anymore.

The closer they got, the more she believed they were meant to be here. Whatever was inside this shroud wanted them here—apparently without their Boxan escorts. She supposed she should have been more worried about that, but if the Drars had wanted them dead, then they would be dead. It was as simple as that. Hicks was still worried though. The career military man didn't like going into a situation there was no escape from.

They were all hands on deck—light years beyond where any Human had gone before.

"Radiation levels are climbing," Zack said.

Kaylan adjusted their approach.

"We're almost to the point of no return," Hicks said.

"I know," Kaylan replied.

The magnetic field shifted during their approach, as if whatever was inside was tracking them.

"Any change from shroud protocols?" Kaylan asked.

"Just trackbacks letting us know they're there," Zack replied.

Kaylan had point on the Athena's controls, and Hicks was her backup if something happened to her. As they approached a patch of space that was seemingly innocuous, the crew of the Athena remained focused on their jobs but kept waiting. Zack had estimated that the shroud had a circumference similar to Saturn's. There were no moons or anything at all in orbit.

Kaylan extended her senses ahead, and her perception of the bridge of the Athena blurred in her mind. She was out beyond the ship, racing headlong into the unknown.

You brought us here. Now let us in, Kaylan thought.

As if in response to her thoughts, a sliver of pale light ignited and quickly spread out. From the recesses of her mind, she heard the others' exclamations at the sight. She even heard Zack call to her and Hicks asking him to be quiet so she could concentrate. A swirling vortex, large enough for the Athena to fit through, opened. Kaylan didn't adjust their speed, trusting that whatever had opened the door for them knew what it was doing.

They went into the vortex.

"Radiation levels have gone way down. It's like we're not out in space anymore. Athena, can you confirm?" Zack asked.

"Sensor diagnostics do not indicate any problems. Minimal atmosphere detected with traces of nitrogen," the AI answered.

Beyond the edge of the shroud, Kaylan saw a megastructure. Playing a hunch, she attempted to adjust their course, but it failed. They were locked on. She pulled her hands away from the console.

"Looks like they're in the driver's seat now," Kaylan said.

"Acknowledged," Hicks said.

"Look at the size of that thing," Zack said. "It's like they built a planet-sized city way out here in deep space."

Kaylan peered at the holoscreen in front of her and magnified the image. "Looks like it's been here a while. Only that place up ahead has power. The rest of it looks brittle, and several areas have collapsed."

Zack came over to them and glanced out the window. One of the long arms that extended away from the center of a structure lost its support and came crashing down. This caused a domino effect for the other squarish buildings in the vicinity. A plume of debris rose and then fell back down.

Kaylan frowned and checked the data pumping in from their sensors. "There is an atmosphere in here, but the composition has too much oxygen for us."

"Not dying from O2 poisoning. Check," Zack said.

"We'll need to suit up for this one," Hicks said and glanced at Zack.

Zack tried to play it off as if he was unimpressed. "You've seen one alien structure, you've seen 'em all. I think I'll stay on the ship this time." He glanced out the window again. "I wonder where the light comes from."

Kaylan followed his gaze. There was light everywhere—not bright sunshine but a place of perpetual twilight. She kept checking the comms channels, but there was nothing. She'd assumed they would have been contacted by now. She glanced around at the ruins of the vast alien city. There was a brownish tinge to most of it, and if she didn't know better, she'd have thought the buildings were rusting. She supposed the high amounts of oxygen in the artificial atmosphere could have caused this over time, but any civilization that could build something like this wouldn't fall victim to oxidation.

They quickly approached the main central structures. The buildings here were made up of harsh angular planes with pyramid-type symmetry. The Athena changed its approach trajectory to a massive central column. Offshoots of the column extended away like the points on a compass.

Kaylan cut the engines, but the Athena kept moving. Large bay doors opened and the Athena went inside the mega structure. The corridors inside could have accommodated tens of thousands of Athena-sized ships. They came to a much smaller chamber, and the Athena descended. The ground beneath them began to glow with an amber-colored light, and the ship came to a stop. Kaylan noted that inside this chamber there was almost no damage to the structure.

"So now what?" Zack asked.

"Now we have a look around," Kaylan said and climbed out of her chair.

"How will we even get down to the ground?" Zack asked.

Hicks glanced out of the window and then brought up the video feed from the port airlock. "Looks like there's a platform waiting for us."

"Great—a platform. How thoughtful of them," Zack said.

They headed for the door to the bridge, but it opened ahead of them. Standing on the other side was Brenda with a very lucid Jonah Redford.

"Hello, Commander," Redford said.

Kaylan gasped and glanced at Brenda. "How?"

Brenda smiled. "I don't know, but as soon as we passed through the shroud, Jonah's symptoms started to improve."

"The brain scans still show damage, but the strokes have stopped, as well as the . . . voices," Redford said.

Kaylan didn't know what to say. She was relieved to see Jonah's improved condition, but she couldn't trust it. "I'm glad you're feeling better. Can you remember anything that's happened?" she asked.

Redford frowned. "It's a bit hazy and jumbled together. Brenda showed me some of the things."

"It has to be this place," Zack said.

"You could be right," Kaylan said.

"We need to decide on the away team," Hicks said.

Redford cleared his throat. "I'd like to come along," he said.

"Absolutely not," Hicks said and looked at Kaylan. "There's no way for us to know if whatever is reversing or halting his condition won't simply stop."

Kaylan pressed her lips together. Her first instinct was to agree with Hicks, but something in Redford's expression gave her pause. He seemed calm and at peace.

"I can't offer you any assurances," Redford said and glanced away. "At least none that *I* would trust anyway."

Kaylan drew in a breath and glanced at the crew of the Athena. "No one stays behind this time. We're all going in."

They met at the port airlock near the shuttle. Kaylan supposed that if there was no safe means to get them to the ground, they could use the shuttle. They all got into their EVA suits. Hicks and Katie had armed themselves. Zack reached inside his locker and withdrew his pulse rifle that Etanu had given him. He gave it a long look, deciding whether or not he wanted to take it with him, and then hung the strap over his shoulder. Hicks looked as if he were about to say something when Katie leaned over and quietly spoke to him. Eventually Hicks gave her a nod.

"Looks like everyone is almost ready. I don't know what we'll find once we leave the ship, but we'll stick together. It doesn't look as if anyone has been here in a long time," Kaylan said.

"I'm not sure if anyone has been here ever," Zack said.

"What do you mean?" Kaylan asked.

"From everything we saw coming in here, it didn't look like anyone actually lived here. There were no vehicles of any kind or anything like that," Zack said.

"He's right," Emma said. "Anyone who actually lived here would have left some sign of life. This place is more like move-in ready, or at least it was at one time."

The crew of the Athena had long gotten used to Zack's keen observations. Kaylan nodded and moved toward the airlock. After receiving an all-clear from the others, she stepped inside. The port airlock could only accommodate five of them at a time, so they split into two groups. Kaylan opened the door to a floating metallic platform just outside. There was no control console or other visible means of control.

"Great, no railings," Zack said.

Kaylan took a step onto the platform, and it felt as if she were stepping onto solid ground. Zack followed her and kept glancing down at his feet. The surface appeared solid, and as she took a closer look, she saw that it was actually swirling as if it was in constant motion. Zack slammed his foot down, hard, and Kaylan jumped.

"Are you crazy?" Kaylan said. "You don't know what that could have done."

Zack looked at her in alarm. "I didn't mean to scare you," he chuckled, "but it doesn't look like I even made a dent. So much for my mighty foot stomp."

Kaylan looked down and saw that Zack was right. The others

joined them, and Hicks closed the door to the Athena so the rest of them could come outside.

"I'm not sure this platform is going to be big enough for everyone," Zack said.

The platform then started spreading, becoming a longer rectangle to accommodate the rest of the crew.

Zack glanced up and let out a nervous laugh. "Ever get the feeling someone is listening to you?"

"Empirical evidence would suggest that we are being monitored," the AI said, its voice coming through the speakers in Kaylan's helmet.

"Thank you, Athena," Zack said. "Are you able to detect them?"

"I've tried several thousand connection attempts using both Human and Boxan protocols, and none of them are working."

"I guess they're not ready to talk to us yet," Zack said.

Kaylan watched as the rest of the crew joined them on the floating platform. Once they had secured the airlock door, the platform began a downward descent. As they reached the ground, the platform hovered above it and then was absorbed into the surface in front of a short path that led inside. Kaylan accessed her suit computer and made sure she could access the shuttle's systems in case they needed to be picked up, but her connections were abruptly severed.

"Zack, can you access the Athena's systems?" Kaylan asked.

Zack frowned for a moment and shook his head. "I'm cut off," he said.

The rest of the crew had the same experience. Kaylan's eyes widened as the Athena pulled away from them and sped off.

"What the hell!" Zack shouted.

"The ship is gone!" Emma cried.

Kaylan glanced at Hicks, who clutched the rifle in his hand. Kaylan tried to raise the Athena on her comms.

"Commander, I'm not able to reach out to you. The control systems are not responding," the AI said.

"What about the shuttle?" Kaylan asked.

"Just locked out," the AI said.

Some of the others groaned.

"Why would they take the ship?" Zack asked.

"To prevent us from leaving," Hicks said.

Kaylan frowned. "I'm not sure. We couldn't leave if we wanted to."

"I don't like that they took the ship," Hicks said in a low voice.

"I don't like it either, but we can't just stay here, waiting for it to come back," Kaylan said.

"Maybe we can find a console inside and figure out where the ship is from there," Zack offered.

There was a loud crash on the far side of the vast chamber as one of the towers collapsed, and Kaylan wondered whether the area they were in would stay standing while they were inside.

"We can't stay here. Let's get moving," Kaylan said.

She strode down the path, and the large door in front of them dissolved. Hicks insisted on going through first, and he did so, keeping his rifle ready. After performing a quick check, he waved the rest of them through. Kaylan could have told him the area was clear but didn't. Just because she couldn't see any other creatures here didn't mean there wasn't something lurking, unseen. After the rest of them had come inside, the door rematerialized behind them. Katie tapped it with her gloved hand and shook her head.

The further they went, the more she thought that Zack's initial observations had been correct. It didn't look like anything had ever lived here. The doorways and corridors were of a size to accommodate a large species like the Boxans, but the plain walls gave no indication of who the Drars actually were. There were no consoles or visible controls for the doors. They were being guided inside, but Kaylan couldn't say for sure where they were being led.

"No, if you detect something, you should tell the rest of the crew. What would you do if I wasn't here?" Zack said.

Kaylan stopped and looked at Zack.

"The AI says there's something on the other side of this wall," Zack said.

"I was merely asking your opinion, Zack," the AI said. "You often point out that I sometimes reveal facts relating to zero percent survivability with no tact."

Zack's brows pushed forward, and Kaylan knew that if he hadn't had a helmet on he would have been rubbing his forehead in consternation.

"Just tell them what you told me," Zack said.

"Faint power source detected beyond this wall," the AI said. "The readings sometimes spike and then disappear altogether."

"Over here?" Kaylan asked, gesturing to the side.

"Affirmative, Commander," the AI said.

Kaylan focused on the wall, but before she could extend her senses, a large portion of the wall evaporated.

"That's so weird," Zack said. "I think I prefer doors that look like doors and open like doors should open."

There was an aqua-colored glow coming from the room beyond. Kaylan stepped inside and rounded the corner. On a large, elevated platform there was a glowing round sphere that seemed to be made up of some type of energy, and it just hovered there with no source visible anywhere. It was the color of transparent cyan, and Kaylan could see through the thing. The sphere itself was the size of a large house. As the crew of the Athena stepped closer, the door rematerialized behind them, but, unlike the other areas, there wasn't anywhere else for them to go.

"Commander, I'm receiving a message," the AI said.

The sphere pulsated as if it were a living entity. Swirling eddies of energy coursed around it.

"Can you translate it?" Kaylan asked.

"No need, I've forwarded the message to all of you, and it should appear on your suit displays now," the AI said.

Kaylan gasped as a single word appeared on her HUD. She glanced at Zack and the others. They were all seeing the same word.

SUBMIT.

CHAPTER TWENTY-THREE

Kladomaor scowled at the main holoscreen. Their sensors had detected trace returns for the Athena, but with their comms systems still down they couldn't open a comms signal to them.

"Do you have them back?" Kladomaor asked.

"Negative, Commander," Triflan said. "It's like they've disappeared."

Kladomaor stood up from his command couch. He wanted to take the biggest weapon he could find and demolish everything in his path. They'd been tracking the Athena's path since the incident.

"Commander, the shroud signal has stopped as well," Triflan said.

The shroud signal had been another surprise, and it had given him enough reason to put other repairs on hold while they raced to catch up with their wayward Human spaceship. He glanced over at Ma'jasalax, but the Mardoxian priestess shook her head.

"Activate scans. I want to know what's in the area. Single sweep only," Kladomaor said.

No need to keep broadcasting their position. They still couldn't go into stealth mode, but he seriously doubted that whatever had knocked them out of the wormhole could be fooled by their stealth technology.

"Take us in, Varek," Kladomaor ordered.

"Acknowledged, Battle Commander," Varek confirmed.

Kladomaor returned to his station. He was still connected to the ship's computer system, and those data feeds still showed information from their sensors. They were at forty percent combat capability, and Kladomaor supposed that was the best they were going to get for a while. There was still work to be done on the Cherubian drive, which was being addressed by his engineering team.

He glanced over at Gaarokk. "What do you make of this?"

"We should be cautious. The Drars led us here for a reason, but they apparently wanted the Humans alone," Gaarokk said.

"There were other ways they could have done this. They didn't have to attack us while in the wormhole," Kladomaor said.

"Perhaps it was a test," Ma'jasalax said.

"Of the Humans?" he asked.

"Of us. Perhaps they were just seeing what we'd do," Ma'jasalax said.

"There's more than a Star Shroud here. This is something else," Kladomaor said.

"I'm counting on it," Ma'jasalax said.

Kladomaor weighed his options. They were closing in fast,

and the area of space that the Athena had disappeared into appeared to be distorted.

"Does the distortion give us any clues as to what's there?" Kladomaor asked.

Gaarokk frowned and looked over at him. "It looks like the entire area resides on the edge of an accretion disk, which is causing the distortion, but it's not truly a distortion. That part of space is out of phase with where we are. Chances are the Athena is just inside it."

"Infinity's Edge," Kladomaor said.

"Until they come out the other side, at least," Gaarokk replied.

Ma'jasalax stopped speaking to Ezerah and came over to them.

"What's Infinity's Edge?" Ezerah asked.

"We use the Cherubian drive to create a wormhole to cross vast distances of the great expanse. If we were to change our trajectory upon entering the wormhole, we would begin to shift from our current position but never reach our destination. No one really knows where those ships go when that happens. They're lost," Gaarokk said.

Ezerah frowned. "But we've changed our trajectory inside wormholes before."

"Correct, but never when we first enter them. It's also the reason why we can't go backward out of a wormhole," Gaarokk said. "If Kladomaor is correct, the Drars were able to utilize this theoretical principle beyond anything we've even conceived of."

"Increased energy readings from the shroud, Battle Commander," Triflan reported.

"On screen," Kladomaor said and focused his attention on

the screen. There was a glowing mass gathering directly in front of them.

"All stop," Kladomaor said.

"Confirmed, Battle Commander," Varek said.

Kladomaor watched the glowing mass and then glanced at Triflan. "Report," he said.

"Energy readings remain steady."

Kladomaor blew out a breath. "Back us away," he said.

He watched as the calculated distance to the shroud increased, and he ordered Varek to stop the ship.

"Energy readings are decreasing," Triflan said.

The glowing mass diminished until they couldn't see it onscreen anymore.

"A warning?" Ma'jasalax said.

Kladomaor nodded. "That's what I was thinking."

"If we can't get any closer without them firing a weapon at us, how are we supposed to help the Athena?" Gaarokk asked.

"I don't know," Kladomaor said, and with each word his scowl deepened.

They circled the shroud, maintaining their distance, but each time they tried to move in closer, the energy readings coming from the shroud spiked.

"I'm not sure how the Athena even made it inside," Gaarokk said.

Kladomaor glanced over at the scientist and waited for him to continue.

"The shroud is surrounded by a powerful magnetic field that should have overwhelmed a ship like the Athena," Gaarokk said.

"There are ways to circumvent that. Perhaps they got in that way. Or they were simply allowed to enter," Kladomaor said.

He scratched the side of his craggy face. There was no way they could get inside. He didn't want to chance trading blows with the Drars. He glanced at the comms station, but there was still no reply to any of their hails. This wasn't the first time they'd come across Drar technology during their search for them, but this was the most complete. Until now, they'd only found pieces, but it seemed that just beyond the shroud was an entire Drar installation.

"We'll have to wait," Ma'jasalax said.

Kladomaor stretched his arms. "How much power could they really have? It was our ancient ancestors who observed the wars involving the Drars. They were the ones who deciphered their message. We should be allowed to go inside, unless . . ."

"The Drars didn't actually build that place," Ma'jasalax said.

Kladomaor gripped the ends of his command couch. The Humans were in trouble. "Battle stations," he said.

The Boxans raced back to their stations.

"I want auxiliary power diverted to the engines," Kladomaor said.

"Acknowledged," Triflan said.

"All ahead full, but be ready to execute evasive maneuvers," Kladomaor said.

"Battle Commander, our weapons systems are still offline," Triflan said.

"I know, and they'll stay that way," Kladomaor said.

The Boxan stealth ship lurched forward in a sudden burst of speed, and the glowing mass immediately returned, gathering in intensity.

"Angle our approach," Kladomaor ordered.

Varek confirmed the order, and Kladomaor watched as the glowing mass followed them along the shroud.

"Bring us in closer," Kladomaor said.

The Boxan ship closed in on the shroud. The glowing mass became a deep orange, and then a molten beam shot toward them.

Varek changed their trajectory and barely dodged the weapon.

"That beam will destroy the ship immediately," Triflan said.

Kladomaor watched as another beam shot toward their ship. Varek changed course again, but the beam grazed the top plating.

"Take us in," Kladomaor said.

"Don't," Ma'jasalax cried. "They're learning our tactics. Each shot gets closer. Withdraw."

Kladomaor clenched his teeth and glared at the holoscreen. Another shot was being primed. "Get us out of here," he said finally.

Varek changed course again, taking them away, and the killing shot never came. The glowing mass faded but kept a bead on the Boxan ship.

They reached the distance they'd been at before his attempt to breach the defenses.

"Battle Commander," Gaarokk said.

Kladomaor looked over at Gaarokk. "What is it?"

"The sensors are showing a slight decrease in diameter of the distortion as a whole," Gaarokk said.

Kladomaor frowned in thought.

"It could be that the energy expended to fire that beam at us could have taxed the system, but without knowing the capacity, we can't be sure how long it would take to drain it fully," Gaarokk said.

Kladomaor nodded. "So they're not completely infallible."

"Should we make another run? See if we can drain the energy some more?" Triflan asked.

Kladomaor scanned through the data on the screen. Varek had done well with evasive maneuvers, but with each shot, the margin of error decreased. He could rotate another helmsman since Varek wasn't the only pilot they had.

"May I have a word with you, please?" Ma'jasalax said.

Kladomaor waved her over, knowing that not listening to Ma'jasalax could cost him more in the long run. He'd also come to rely on the Mardoxian priestess's insights.

"You shouldn't do this," Ma'jasalax said quietly. "Kaylan and the others are inside, and we don't know what will happen to them inside if we continue to—"

"Contact, Battle Commander," Triflan announced.

Kladomaor swung his gaze to the holoscreen but didn't see anything coming from the Drar installation.

"It's coming from behind us, Battle Commander," Triflan said.

A secondary display appeared on screen, showing the contact that the AI had assigned the designation alpha.

"Varek, bring us around. Passive scans only," Kladomaor said.

"Passive scan burst initiated," Triflan said.

Kladomaor and the rest of the crew on the bridge waited. Fighting wars in space involved a lot of waiting before an actual engagement occurred, but an effective commander almost never rushed in—at least not the ones who lived long. There were times to take that gamble, such as he'd done with the shroud, and he'd come away having learned something about his adversary.

"Xiiginn contact, Battle Commander, scout class ship," Triflan said.

Kladomaor narrowed his gaze and was relieved that it wasn't a Xiiginn warship out there hunting for them. Without stealth, they stood no chance against a warship, even one with a poor commander, but a Xiiginn scout ship with full weapons capability still had the capacity to take them out. Xiiginn High Command must not have been wholly convinced they had escaped from the asteroid space station, but Mar Arden undoubtedly convinced them to send a scout ship to track them. Kladomaor rubbed the tips of his fingers together while he was thinking. The mere thought of Mar Arden was enough to ignite his anger, but he couldn't allow that to affect his judgment. The lives of his fellow Boxans and that of the Human crew of the Athena were all depending on him. He couldn't assume Mar Arden was aboard that ship.

"Hold our current position," Kladomaor said.

Gaarokk looked at him questioningly. Since the scientist had been with Kladomaor for so long, he sometimes forgot that Gaarokk wasn't familiar with military tactics.

"Our stealth capabilities are damaged, and we have limited combat capability, so meeting our enemy head-on isn't our best choice. They may have tracked us here, but I'm willing to wager that their commander has stumbled a lot along the way, given that our trek here wasn't a straight shot through a wormhole," Kladomaor said.

"Do they see us?" Gaarokk asked.

"Not yet. While active scans would certainly reveal our position, we do have some cover from the distortion field of the Drar installation. I think they'll be preoccupied with that," Kladomaor said.

"What are you going to do?"

"We wait. We'll hold this position and see what they're going to do."

"You don't mean to attack them?"

"Oh, we'll attack them. Just not yet. Attacking them now at this range would better serve them than us. We cannot allow them the slightest chance to get access to the Drar installation," Kladomaor said.

Gaarokk frowned in thought. "Why not allow them to approach and let the Drar weapons system we've been dodging finish them off?"

"We can't."

"Why not?"

"Because the crew of the Athena is inside that thing, and we don't know what will happen to those inside if we continue to drain the energy from it. Don't forget, if this truly is of Drar origin, it has had many cycles in the great expanse and could very well be at the end of its lifecycle," Kladomaor said.

Gaarokk nodded. "Battle Commander," he acknowledged as a show of respect.

Kladomaor continued to weigh his options, but all he could really do at the moment was wait to see what that Xiiginn scout ship would do next. They were still quite far out, and he had the sneaking suspicion that the crew of the Athena needed all the time he could give them.

CHAPTER TWENTY-FOUR

Michael Hunsicker had thought he'd be able to relax once they reached the lunar base. After all the work he and Chazen had put into the life pod, he was looking forward to taking it easy for a short while before returning to Earth— nothing extensive in terms of time off but just enough to catch his breath. Michael was far from averse to hard work, but they had hardly stopped working since they'd arrived at the lunar base. Chazen could go for extended periods of time without rest, but Michael was reaching his limits. Alissa Archer had offered him sleeping quarters, but Michael wasn't sure it would be a good idea to leave Chazen at this point. The Boxan was most comfortable with him, and Michael didn't want him to feel that he had abandoned him. As a compromise, Alissa had a cot brought to the office that was connected to the secondary command and control room where they were working and told him to get some sleep.

With the help of lunar base personnel, they'd made quick

work of extracting the Boxan equipment and setting it up, and Chazen had agreed to let the engineers examine the materials they'd used for the life pod. One of the first things Chazen had set up was the specialized communications equipment he'd brought along that would allow him to transmit the self-destruct sequence to the Boxan listening station on Pluto. The anomaly detected well beyond Pluto's orbit appeared to have gone quiet.

Michael had snagged a few hours' sleep and sat up on the cot, rubbing his eyes. A loud yawn escaped his lips, and he glanced out the office window to see if anyone had noticed. No one had. Most people were still enamored with their exalted guest. He looked at Chazen, who was busy answering questions, and the deep resonance of the Boxan's voice carried all the way to the office. Michael stood up and stretched. He wouldn't have minded a shower, but he didn't know where they were.

Alissa glanced over in his direction and, seeing that he was awake, walked over to the office. She checked her watch as she came inside. "It's only been about four hours since you went to sleep," she said. She took in his appearance with a quizzical brow that reminded him of Kathryn. "I think we can get you a change of clothes and perhaps a shower. If you play your cards right, maybe a hot meal," she said with a wink and led him out of the office.

Michael followed and then lingered in the doorway. He cast a furtive glance at Chazen. "Those all sound great, but I'm not sure I should leave him."

Alissa followed his gaze. "He'll be okay. I think the more he interacts with us the more comfortable he becomes. Come on."

Michael followed Alissa from the room. She was an older woman in her fifties, and her dark hair had hints of gray. She walked with an air of confidence that seemed to take hold of the people around her.

Alissa glanced back at him. "You're not that old. Keep up," she said.

Michael chuckled and quickened his pace to catch up with her.

"What was the Boxan listening station like?" Alissa asked.

"It was incredible. It made us all feel like we were little kids because it was designed for Boxans," Michael said.

"They're not exactly small. I reviewed the Athena mission update file from Kaylan Farrow before you arrived. NASA ordered me locked in a room so I could be brought up to speed. Kaylan was your second in command?" Alissa asked.

"That's right, although after all they've been through, I'm not sure I would want to be in command of that. She's exceptional," Michael said.

"Most women in NASA are," Alissa said.

She led him to the showers on base. Unisex. There were no societal expectations for things like separate bathrooms when one worked and lived off-planet, but it wasn't as if the stalls were out in the open, so there was some measure of privacy. Alissa told him to use one of the showers while she went to get him a change of clothes.

"Should have done this after you arrived," Alissa said, and then Michael heard her leave the room.

Michael turned the water on and stepped into the hot flow. He squeezed his eyes shut and just stood there, relishing the feel of it. The tension left his neck and shoulders as he cocked his head from side to side. He wasn't one for taking long showers, but he didn't want to leave. The only thing that would be better than this would be swimming in the warm turquoise waters of Bermuda. He and his late wife, Kathryn, had taken long strolls on the legendary pink sandy beaches. They'd returned to Bermuda as often as they could over the years, and for the longest time Michael hadn't even considered returning there. Too many memories, he'd told himself, but he found that he didn't feel that way anymore. It had taken a long journey to Pluto and back for him to finally lay his late wife to rest. He still missed her, and the pang in his chest and the back of his eyes was still there when he thought of her, but he was more at peace with it than he'd ever been before.

The door to the outer room opened, and Alissa announced that she'd laid out some clothes for him to change into when he was finished.

"I'll wait outside because I know how you older fellas can get," Alissa joked.

Michael laughed and a few minutes later turned the water off. Jets of air blew the water off his body and dried his skin. There were no towels because water must be conserved, especially on the moon. He saw that Alissa had left a shaving kit for him and put it to good use. The clothes Alissa had brought him fit well enough and were comfortable. He looked like every other person on the base. He glanced at himself in the mirror and pressed his lips together. He could use a haircut, but there wasn't anything he could do about it now.

Alissa smiled at him as he came out. "You clean up nice, Commander."

"Thanks," Michael said.

"Let's see about getting you some real food instead of whatever it was that you've been eating."

"Rations and something Chazen adapted for me."

She led him to the mess hall, and Michael helped himself to some roasted chicken and vegetables. He and Alissa were pretty much left alone while they both quietly ate. It had been months since he'd had real food.

"I'm surprised your resident doctor hasn't been banging down your door to get me into an exam room," Michael said.

Alissa smiled knowingly. "Oh, they tried, but Houston told them to give you some space."

Michael finished eating and was starting to feel himself becoming sleepy again, so he stood up and deposited his tray in the receptacle.

"We should head back," Alissa said. "Do you have any thoughts on Chazen?"

"He's a good . . . guy. I wouldn't be here if it weren't for him. Why do you ask?"

"His presence here is unprecedented. We fully intend to honor the asylum agreement we have with him, but I was asked to provide a preliminary evaluation. He was a bit quiet when he first got here, but that's understandable considering the circumstances. I get the impression, though, that Boxans don't find themselves in need of other people's help very often," Alissa said.

Michael snorted. "You got that right. He's been alone for a long time. I didn't press him very hard for personal information, and I have no idea who he may have left behind on his home planet."

Alissa nodded. "If the rest of the Boxans are like him, they're a dedicated bunch. He spent over sixty years in isolation for his culture. I don't know if I could have done that—or anyone, for that matter."

"He wasn't awake for all of that. He spent large portions of his time in suspended animation."

"Stasis," Alissa said. "Now that *is* interesting. I'm not sure how I'd feel about sleeping my life away."

"Me either," Michael agreed.

They came to the secondary command and control room where they'd left Chazen, and the room was abuzz with activity. Michael and Alissa hastened over to where Chazen was. The Boxan sat on the floor with his back against the wall, and the other people in the room were all talking at once.

"What happened?" Alissa asked.

"There was another anomaly detected, but this one was much closer to Earth," a man named Stevens answered.

Stevens went to one of the consoles and brought up the main wall screen. A Boxan's face Michael had never seen before was onscreen.

"Humans of Earth," the Boxan said, "I am called Prax'pedax. We come here at the behest of the Humans aboard the Athena, and we want you to know that you are not alone in the threat against the Xiiginn."

Michael's eyes widened. The Boxan onscreen looked much older than Chazen and more vigorous, as if he were of some type of warrior-class Boxan that Michael had never seen before. He felt his eyes become misty, and he went to Chazen's side.

"They've come for you," Michael said.

Chazen's large features were awash with emotions—too many and too intense for Michael to accurately count. How does one act after seeing another of their own kind for the first time in sixty years? Michael was pretty sure he wouldn't have been able to stay on his feet either.

CHAPTER TWENTY-FIVE

E dward Johnson would rather have been at Mission
Control in Houston, Texas. Instead, he was back at
NORAD under the watchful eyes of General Sheridan. Over the
past few weeks, he and the general had come to an uneasy understanding. Ed had no doubt that if the general could, he'd lock Ed
away and throw away the key. But Ed's presence at NORAD was
under presidential authority. To give Ed the gravitas needed,
she'd made him one of her special advisors to the president. Presidential authority and the presence of Iris Barrett were enough to
irritate the old general. A couple of the general's subordinates
had believed they could strong-arm Iris, away from watchful
eyes. Those men were still recovering from the damage Ed's
assistant had done to them.

Despite all the legwork Dux Corp had put into the Earth
Coalition Force, the nations of the world were picking it over
and dissecting it at a snail's pace, piece by piece. It had taken
three tries for the US government to make basic universal health-

care available to all its citizens—three attempts and several near collapses of the global economy. At this moment, it felt that those historic events had happened much quicker than the UN adopting the creation of the ECF. If the nations tried to meet the threat of the Xiiginns divided, there was little hope that they could survive. Ed wanted more than anything to avoid a future where billions of people perished because the governments of the world couldn't agree on how they were going to defend the Earth from a hostile alien attack force.

The presence of the Boxans was a stroke of good fortune, but the people of Earth shouldn't be looking to the Boxans for direction in governing their planet. The dominion of Earth had to stay entirely within Human control if they were to have a future.

Iris leaned in toward his ear. "Five minutes."

The general watched him, and when Colonel Hines announced the same information, the general seemed to snort to himself.

"One day we'll have to find your source in the White House," Sheridan said.

Ed smiled. "We're on the same side, General. I hope you can believe that."

At that moment, the holoscreens went live, and President Susan Halloway appeared. On one of the other screens, the image of several Boxans was displayed, but it was the one called Prax'pedax that caught his attention. He was the one Kaylan had said would come. There were two Boxan ships heading toward the moon at this very moment.

"Thank you for agreeing to meet with us, Prax'pedax," President Halloway said.

"I'd like to make a few statements to your species," Prax'pedax said.

Ed kept watching the Boxan with a sense of awe that they were actually communicating with an alien species that in many ways was beyond anything imagined on Earth.

"We'll listen to what you have to say," the president said.

"I hope so, for all our sakes. As you know, I've personally met the crew of the Athena. It was because of that meeting and at the behest of a close friend that I am here before your species today. We are here to help Earth defend itself from the Xiiginns using your current technology. We will not share advancements that you weren't already on the road to discovering for yourselves," Prax'pedax said.

"I'm not sure I'm following what you're saying. It's my understanding that you've already shared some of your technology with us and put us on the path that led us where we are today. Will that not continue in the face of the Xiiginn threat?" President Halloway asked.

"As I've said, we will help you harden your lines of defense where the Xiiginns are concerned, and if they do come here, we will help defend the Earth with the use of our ships," Prax'pedax said.

The area around General Sheridan lit up, signifying that he wanted to speak.

"Go ahead, General," President Halloway said.

"We appreciate your offer of assistance, but wouldn't it be prudent to help us build ships of our own so we can learn to defend ourselves?" Sheridan asked.

"Perhaps in time," Prax'pedax said.

This response drew a lot of comments from people around the war room in NORAD, as well as those virtually connected.

"I'm afraid that's not good enough," Sheridan said.

Prax'pedax looked surprised at this response, and Ed had to admit that at this moment he was glad Sheridan was in the position he was in.

"The way I see it, the Xiiginns only know about our planet because you led them here. Your listening station sent one of our ships across the galaxy, putting her crew in harm's way. So for you to come here and say you'll help is a step in the right direction, but what happens to us if you decide to leave or are defeated by the Xiiginns?" Sheridan asked.

Prax'pedax drew in a patient breath. "I understand your concerns. They are admirable, and I can find no fault in the arguments you've raised. Our war with the Xiiginns has been a long one, and it has cost us dearly. Rest assured that neither myself or any Boxan here with me will abandon you to face the Xiiginns alone."

President Halloway came to prominence on screen, and Prax'pedax's gaze shifted to her. "You should know there are other nations on our planet proposing that we meet the Xiiginns at the negotiating table."

Prax'pedax's large flaxen eyes narrowed menacingly. "That would be unfortunate."

"How?"

"Should you meet with the Xiiginns, they will fill your minds with empty promises while they put a shackle around each and every Human on this planet. We've seen them do it to other species—give them technology they're not ready to control and exploit them for resources," Prax'pedax said.

"What kind of resources? Perhaps if we negotiate with them, they'll deal with us peacefully," Dr. Gray asked.

Ed scowled and wished he could send Iris to make that idiot close his mouth.

Prax'pedax leveled his gaze. "The Xiiginns give the appearance of humble offers, but if you let them in, they will ruin your world. The Nershals, a species once again in alliance with us, have learned this firsthand. They've been recently fighting the Xiiginns to get them to leave their star system."

Gray flipped through several documents on his tablet. "Yes, the report from the Athena has it right here. Genetic experimentation was being performed on Nershals. It also says that the Nershals authorized such experiments, so I'm a bit confused as to whether the Nershals are the best example to use."

"Somebody shut this idiot up," Ed growled.

Dr. Gray's mouth rounded in shock.

"The Boxans come here to offer us help and you play political games with them?" Ed said.

"I don't believe I asked for your input. Your time will come, and you'll end up in a cell," Gray said.

"I'll see to it that you end up in a place much worse," Ed said, sneering.

There were a few tense moments as people regained control of their flaring tempers. Suddenly, a sharp sound erupted from Prax'pedax, and Ed had the distinct impression that the Boxan was laughing at them.

President Halloway cleared her throat. "I must apologize. As you can see, there are many differing viewpoints of these events and a good deal of fear about our future. Perhaps you could give us more details about your intentions—what kind of ships you've brought. That sort of thing."

Ed admired Susan Halloway. She was firm when the situation called for it, but she also knew how to calm down those around her.

"We've brought three ships of the wall, Dreadnaught class, capable of providing adequate coverage of your star system. If the Xiiginns come with an invasion force, they'll bring their warships, along with support ships for a long engagement and occupation of your system," Prax'pedax said.

"And just three of your Dreadnaught ships can stand against all of that?" Halloway asked.

"As any veteran of war will tell you, one weapons system is not equal to another. The Xiiginns enjoy a numerical advantage, but what they lack are great tacticians. For example, Kladomaor used his stealth ship to stand against three Xiiginn warships using superior tactics," Prax'pedax said.

General Sheridan cleared his throat. "Superior tactics will only get you so far, but it sounds to me that the fighting force you've brought, along with anything we can muster, will only slow down a real invasion force. Granted that at this moment I don't have the details that are available to you."

Prax'pedax gave the general a nod of respect. "We will share that tactical information with you in order to put up the best defense possible for your species. You are correct. Three ships, even Dreadnaught class, are not enough to protect your star system indefinitely."

"How would you suggest we defend ourselves indefinitely so the Xiiginns will go away?" Sheridan asked.

"You'll learn, you'll adapt, and perhaps you'll overcome," Prax'pedax said.

Ed indicated that he wanted the floor, and Sheridan nodded for him to take it.

"I have a question for you. There has to be a compelling reason for the Xiiginns to come here in such force. We possess something that is highly valued, both by you and the Xiiginns. Is that correct?" Ed asked.

Prax'pedax regarded him for a moment. "You're referring to the evidence that the Mardoxian trait exists within Humans?"

"I am," Ed said.

There was quiet murmuring both by the people near him and elsewhere.

"We've brought our own representative from the Mardoxian sect with us to further validate that claim," Prax'pedax said.

"Just so everyone is on the same page," Ed said, "the sources you were referencing earlier are some of the reasons the Xiiginns are coming here. They may want access to our DNA and other things, but it's this trait they really want. What I would like to know is, what lengths are you authorized to take to keep the Xiiginns from gaining access to that trait?" Ed asked.

A solemn silence took hold of everyone on the call, including the Boxans.

"Regarding authorized actions," Prax'pedax began, "the mandate that brings me here is one of mutual benefit to both our species. I have a certain amount of freedom with which to carry out that mandate, and at the same time I will do what I need to do to preserve my own species."

Ed felt his mouth go dry. "I sincerely hope it never comes to that." He glanced over at General Sheridan. "I have no further questions."

The rest of the call went into logistics, aligning various teams that would meet with Boxan emissaries once they reached Earth. While Ed did pay attention, his thoughts kept going over Prax'pedax's response to his questions.

"Are you alright, Ed? You look a bit shaken up," Iris said after the meeting.

"I am . . . a bit shaken up."

"About what?"

"The Boxans basically said that if they, or we, can't figure out a way to defend ourselves against the Xiiginns, they'll destroy our species just to keep the Xiiginns from using us in their own war with the Boxans," Ed said.

Iris blew out a breath. "Talk about being stuck between a rock and a hard place."

Ed sighed. "Yeah," he said. "We knew this was coming, but Prax'pedax made it all the more real for everyone."

Iris regarded him for a moment. "The question needed to be asked. We needed to know the stakes."

"I know. I think part of me wanted to be wrong," Ed said.

Iris smiled. "That doesn't happen that often . . . or ever as far as I know. Come on. I see that Sheridan wants to speak with you."

CHAPTER TWENTY-SIX

S *UBMIT.*
The word appeared on the heads-up display of Zack's helmet. He looked at the others and they'd all been stunned into silence. "Athena, are you sure this isn't a botched translation?"

"Negative. That data was transmitted in clear text," the AI replied.

"Let's not panic. Perhaps it thinks it's sending us a greeting," Kaylan said.

The glowing sphere continued to pulsate with energy.

"How would it even know our language? The Boxans studied us for a long time, so they had time to figure it out," Emma said.

She paced over to the side, never taking her eyes from the sphere. A rectangular image of the Athena's approach to the shroud appeared on the sphere itself.

Zack's mouth hung open in astonishment. Whatever it was could hear them. "How long could they have been watching us?" he asked.

He was more giving voice to his thoughts than asking an actual question, but the image on the sphere began to change. The crew of the Athena watched as the events that had brought them here were shown to them as if they were watching a cosmic rewind. The images went by so fast that they began to blur together until they came to a stop on a picture of the Athena next to Kladomaor's ship, heading toward the asteroid space station.

Zack glanced at Kaylan. "How is this possible?"

The images blanked out on the sphere.

SUBMIT.

The word appeared on the sphere now. Zack shifted his grip on the pulse rifle and resisted the urge to open fire on it. Any species that could have brought them here knew which word they were showing them.

Kaylan stepped away from them, moving toward the sphere. "Are you the Drars?" she asked.

A three-dimensional hologram appeared beside Kaylan of an alien Zack had never seen before. The thick, corded muscles reminded him of the complex root network of an old tree. Its skin colors were a mixture of grays and browns, with a tinge of mossy green. The alien looked like it could have made a home in a swampy jungle, and Zack would never know it was there. The small eyes were midway on its elongated head. The alien was hunched, as if it could easily move on both of its legs or use its long, powerful arms to propel itself forward. It almost reminded Zack of a protokar, but not quite. The alien didn't look like it had a mouth, and if it did, it was hidden behind the bearded tentacles that adorned its elongated head. The hologram slowly turned around, showing the creature's thick body. It was easily the size of a Boxan. Tentacles corded together to the ends of its arms, which Zack guessed were the creature's hands.

"Are the Drars here?" Kaylan asked.

More holograms appeared, but all showed the Drar facedown on the ground. The holograms disappeared and the sphere showed a depiction of the galaxy—a vast ocean of stars and a rapid expansion of star systems, all shown in different colors. Spaceships, unlike anything they'd ever seen before, were shown going out into an expanding universe. Eventually, spaceships gave way to planetoid ships moving through the galaxy. A multitude of lifeforms flashed with each new star system. There were so many of them that Zack started to squint his eyes. Then the images on the sphere began to change, showing wars and battles being fought. At first, the images were of the Drars fighting amongst themselves. Then the confrontations spread to include ships. Planetoid spaceships were left in heaping wrecks. Eventually the war escalated, and bright flashes of entire star systems were snuffed out. The war spread throughout the galaxy, and the Drar empire fractured.

"This must be what the Boxans saw," Zack said.

The images on the sphere all ceased at once for a moment, then showed a view from the bridge of a ship of a lone green planet orbiting a single star system. The planet had four moons, and the images shifted to show Boxans caring for the forests and vast grasslands of the planet, their instinct for putting their world in order present early in their culture.

The images came to a stop, and the sphere returned to its translucent aqua color.

"I think we just saw a condensed version of the history of our galaxy," Zack said.

"Or they could be showing us what we expected to see," Hicks said.

"I didn't expect to see that," Zack said.

"Whatever this place is, something here has been watching us for a long time. The Drars aren't here. I think it's time for us to start looking for a way to get out of here," Hicks said.

Kaylan pressed her lips together in thought and then glanced back at the sphere. "Where is our ship?" she asked.

An image of the Athena appeared in some type of dock. There were many machines seeming to form from liquid metal all around it, and they were all over the ship, including inside.

"What are they doing to our ship?" Zack asked.

"I'm not quite—" the AI started to say and was cut off.

"Say again, Athena," Zack said.

There was no reply, not even from the satellite versions of the AI that resided on their suit computers. Zack's mouth went dry. The AI was one of them, and to have it suddenly gone was ominous.

Hicks stepped toward the sphere and lowered his rifle. "How far away from us is our ship?"

The image of the Athena being swarmed by liquid metal machines became smaller, and a bright yellow line traced its way past buildings, coming to a stop where they were.

"I don't know the scale of this, but that looked really far," Zack said.

"It's not looking good," Hicks agreed.

"We don't even know what we're doing here," Emma said.

"She's right," Kaylan said. "There has to be a reason we're here." She turned and faced the sphere. "What is this place?"

The sphere showed another image of the galaxy that seemed

to have gone quiet. There were no more star systems popping out of existence. The perspective zoomed in to show machines repairing the remnant pieces of a planetoid ship. Smaller devices circled around it and were joined in a network that Zack guessed was something similar to the Star Shroud. A blazing truth pushed forward in his mind.

"I know what this place is," Zack said suddenly, and the others looked at him. "This place was supposed to be a refuge."

"For whom?" Hicks asked.

"The Drars. It doesn't look like they built it, but the bulk of their knowledge was in everything they built. Why not an AI or something else that was preconfigured to preserve itself, you know? Like an onboard auto-repair cycle for a ship system, but in this case, it built this for when the Drars return," Zack said, looking at Kaylan. "I know it sounds crazy, but given what we just saw, it seems to fit. What do you guys think?"

Kaylan blew out a breath. "I know enough not to dismiss your ideas out of hand."

"Agreed, but this place is falling apart," Hicks said.

"Maybe it's had enough and knows the Drars aren't coming, or maybe the Drars who were here died. This place could only be working within the confines of its programming," Zack said.

"I want us to go back to the ship. I want to know if that thing is showing us the truth," Hicks said.

The doorway behind them dematerialized, and Zack used his implants to try and find the Athena's AI, but it wouldn't respond.

"The way is open. Let's get out of here," Hicks said.

Zack headed toward the door and the others began to follow. He waited for Kaylan. She'd taken a step toward him and then stopped, turning back toward the sphere. Zack glanced over to the side and saw Redford there, watching the sphere with his mouth agape. Hicks called over to Zack from outside the room.

"Are you coming?" Zack asked Kaylan.

"I'll be right there," Kaylan said.

Zack walked through the doorway, and it started to rematerialize behind him. He watched in horror as Kaylan was stuck on the other side. He stuck his hand out, hoping it would stop the door from reforming, but the skin on his hand turned icy cold and he cried out, snatching it back. The door became solid, and he slammed his fist on it, crying out Kaylan's name.

"What happened?" Hicks said.

"They're stuck in there," Zack said.

Hicks's eyes widened, and he took a quick head count. "Kaylan is in there with Jonah and Brenda."

Zack put his face by the door. "Can you hear me?" he shouted.

He placed his ear on the cool surface of the door but didn't hear any reply.

Hicks tried to get them on comms, but there was no reply. "Come on. We'll search for another way in," he said.

Zack looked at the door, unable to believe what had just happened. He raised the pulse rifle and took aim.

"No, don't," Hicks said and placed his hand on top of the rifle, gently forcing it back down. "We don't want to antagonize this thing."

"Well, this thing is antagonizing me. Why is it separating us?" Zack asked.

"Your guess is as good as mine. Come on. Staying here isn't going to help anything," Hicks said.

Zack took one last glance at the door and followed Hicks

and the others. He kept going over what had happened. What could it want from Kaylan, and why cut off the Athena's AI? He could rationalize being cut off from the AI if the image of what was happening to the Athena was true, in which case them rushing off to find their ship wasn't going to help. But there should still be a portable version of the AI in their suit computers, and Zack used his implants to try and find it. Even when he'd been trapped in the pit, the AI had still been with him.

Zack turned his mind away from the missing AI and back to the sphere. SUBMIT. What did it want from them?

"Why didn't it talk to us?" Zack asked.

Emma, who happened to be walking next to him, glanced over. "What do you mean?"

"The sphere or whatever is in control here. It understands what we're saying, and the text message shows that it at least knows one word of our language. Why didn't it talk to us?" Zack asked.

"I'm actually not surprised that it didn't talk to us," Emma said.

"Really?" he asked and glanced back toward the door, hoping it would be open.

"I think you're right that there's some kind of AI here, and one thing you've taught me is that an AI will try to be as efficient as possible when attempting to achieve a specific task. Speaking is a primitive form of communication," Emma said.

Zack snorted. "I thought girls liked to talk," he said and glanced over at Hicks.

Emma frowned. "This thing chose to communicate with images, and it conveyed a lot of information that way. Wouldn't you agree?"

"I guess, but we would have learned more if it had just talked to us instead of making us guess what it wants," Zack said.

"That's just it. I don't think that's the case. If it had talked to us, we would have bombarded it with questions, some of which probably wouldn't have been useful."

Zack blew out a breath. "This reminds me of being a kid and having someone not explain things fully to me."

Emma laughed. "That's a pretty good comparison."

Zack shook his head. "So, another species of galactic parents is trying to glean something from us, only we don't know what they want or whether their intentions are good or bad."

"If their intentions were bad, wouldn't you think something bad would have already happened?" Emma asked.

"I guess . . . I mean, I hope their intentions are good, but one thing I've learned is that everyone has their own agenda, and I'm just wondering what part we're playing in theirs," Zack said.

"Now you're making *me* start to worry," Emma said.

Zack couldn't help it. He was inclined to be suspicious of nearly everything, which was one of the things that made him an excellent hacker. Now he just needed to figure out what they could do here in a place they didn't understand so they could get Kaylan and the others back.

CHAPTER TWENTY-SEVEN

Prax'pedax sat on the command couch of a massive Dreadnaught-class starship, one of three they'd brought from the colony fleet. Veteran Boxan soldiers serving aboard these ships had been drawn from the remnant forces that had escaped the asteroid research base. The home fleet was engaged with the Xiiginns in the Nerva star system, attempting to free the Nershals from Xiiginn control. The Nerva star system had become a new battlefront in an old war. Boxans didn't procreate as fast as the other species they'd encountered in the great expanse, so the loss of any Boxan soldier was compounded by the fact that it took so long for a new soldier to take their place.

His green battlemesh shirt was adorned with golden rings at the shoulders, signifying his status as Battle Leader for this force. The bridges of the Dreadnaught-class ship were much larger than the cruiser-class ships he'd served on. The fact that Home Fleet had dispatched three of these ships to the star system that was home to the Humans was a testament of great honor for this young species.

Prax'pedax glanced over at Thesulia, a priestess of the Mardoxian sect. She wore the brown ceremonial robes that marked her as a priestess. Nearby was a Boxan who called himself Kray. He was Thesulia's protector, and should the need arise, he'd be her executioner to prevent the Mardoxian priestess from falling into Xiiginn hands.

Prax'pedax's encounter with the Humans had so far left him unimpressed. As a planetary society, they were still fighting amongst themselves, but Kladomaor's transmission had counseled patience when dealing with them, and his old friend's word was the only reason he'd come here to begin with.

"I'd like to hear your opinion about the Humans now that you've gotten a chance to listen to some of them speak," Prax'pedax said.

Thesulia regarded him for a moment. "I found some of them to be quite shrewd. They've had some time to put those questions together, and the fact that they're thinking in those terms indicates that at least some of them believe the threat of the Xiiginns is real."

"What did Ma'jasalax's report say?" Prax'pedax asked.

Not even he could read the reports between Mardoxian priestesses. Thesulia's ears twitched, causing her thick braids to move.

"I'm just looking for an insight into dealing with the Humans," Prax'pedax said.

"An honest approach is best. They don't trust us, and I can hardly fault them for that."

"They believe we're the reason they're in danger in the first place," Prax'pedax said.

"Are they wrong?" Thesulia asked.

This was one of the reasons he found the Mardoxian priestess so frustrating. Her presence on the bridge was that of an advisor, but there were times he felt as if he were answering to her instead of his superiors at the colony.

Due to the Boxans' initial failure to ally with the Nershals against the Xiiginns, Prax'pedax never thought the Nershals would change their allegiance and join the Boxans. In fact, he had gone on record to the High Council when it reviewed Kladomaor's request for his unorthodox approach to expose the Xiiginn's evil practices before the Nershals went the way of the Qegi race and became extinct. Kladomaor had proven him wrong, and it had left Prax'pedax wondering what else they'd been wrong about.

"Perhaps you didn't like them figuring out that if we fail to prevent this system from being taken over by the Xiiginns, we'll destroy it," Thesulia said.

"That is our mandate," Prax'pedax said.

"Only if you follow it. We can't expect the Humans to trust us if they suspect that we'll destroy them if they were to ally with the Xiiginns. Such policies will push them into the Xiiginns' arms, and that would be a fate much worse for everyone," Thesulia said.

"What would you suggest I do then? I thought I was being honest with them."

"You were, but the mandate itself is wrong. In some respects, do the opposite of the mandate. Allow the Humans to come aboard our ships. Let them see how we work. They need to believe we'll fight side by side with them. Earn their trust and be willing to sacrifice Boxan lives for it. Only then can both our species stand against the Xiiginns," Thesulia said.

Prax'pedax regarded the Mardoxian priestess for a few moments while he considered what she had said. "If I were to do as you suggest, there could be criminal charges brought against me. My second in command would be compelled to take over the whole operation."

"Are you not the Battle Leader of this group? Lead then. Win them over to the proper path . . . the only path that has a chance of ensuring the survival of our species," Thesulia said.

Prax'pedax stood and stepped down from the command couch. "This would go against all established protocols and could be a disservice to the Humans."

"They'll adapt. I've conferred with others of the sect, and we're in agreement with this course of action."

Prax'pedax frowned. "Why not take this before the High Council?"

"Sometimes the council needs a strong nudge in order to bring about much-needed change."

"Did one of those nudges come in the form of a Battle Commander named Kladomaor?"

Thesulia smiled. "Among others."

"When did the sect become a political force?" Prax'pedax asked.

Thesulia leveled a solemn gaze at him. "Since the loss of Sethion and all those we left behind."

Prax'pedax blew out a breath that ended in a low growl. Many still believed that the loss of their homeworld, Sethion, signified the downfall of the Boxans.

"Alright, I'll think about changing our approach," he said after some hesitation.

"I suggest you contact them through the newly formed Earth Coalition Force. Make the Humans unite as much as they can in order to give them the best possible chance for their survival."

"Perhaps I should ask you to speak to them. Convince them that we're here to help."

Thesulia glanced over at the large holoscreen displaying the bright blue planet the Humans called Earth. "They wouldn't listen to me any better than they've listened to you. Our actions will convince them of our intentions, but you need to fix your botched first meeting with them by extending them an invitation."

"I can't secure this star system and play diplomat at the same time."

"Then why did you come?"

Prax'pedax glanced at the other Boxans on the bridge. They were all busy working at their stations, pointedly ignoring the conversation going on around them. "Perhaps you should go to the planet's surface and deal with the Humans directly."

Thesulia seemed amused by this. "In time, but not now."

"Why not now?" he asked and watched as her expression became distant.

He'd seen the Mardoxian priestess work before, and while he highly respected her and knew that she represented the next step on their species' evolutionary journey, he was also wary of her.

Prax'pedax returned to the command couch. "Comms, open up a channel to the Earth Coalition Force."

"They've provided us with official contacts for the individual nations, but not the actual ECF," his comms officer, Wynog, answered.

"Then utilize the contacts we've got and tell them we'd like to meet the ECF," Prax'pedax said.

"At once," Wynog said.

Prax'pedax waited as various communications went out.

"Incoming comms from an installation on their moon. It's Boxan," Wynog said.

Prax'pedax frowned, and Thesulia came to stand at his side. "Put them through," he said.

A Boxan's face appeared on the holoscreen. "I am Chazen of the Star Shroud team tasked with studying the Humans."

Prax'pedax's eyes widened. "We had no idea there were any Boxans in this system."

Chazen's eyes narrowed. "That's impossible. I followed protocol. I sent my initial status report to Sethion and shut down all communications after that, waiting for a transport ship to come."

Prax'pedax glanced at Thesulia, but she continued to watch the Boxan onscreen. He couldn't believe what he was hearing. Prax'pedax softened his expression. "Sethion fell shortly after the decree to shut down all Star Shrouds to prevent them from falling into Xiiginn hands."

He watched as the Boxan onscreen took in the news that their home planet had fallen.

"Sethion is . . . gone?" Chazen asked.

"It's . . ." Prax'pedax began.

"It's in quarantine," Thesulia said. "There are orbital platforms to prevent anyone from leaving or making it to the surface. The Xiiginns made it to Sethion and used their influence to cause a massive civil war. We've been searching for a way to cure Xiiginn compulsion ever since."

Chazen looked away from the screen, unable to speak.

Prax'pedax looked at Thesulia. "How many like him were left stranded in alien star systems? How many did the High Council abandon? How many!" Prax'pedax shouted.

"Too many," Thesulia answered. "Now you know why the Mardoxian sect began to influence the direction of the High Council."

"How could they have left all those Boxans stranded? Do they know?" Prax'pedax asked.

Thesulia's gaze hardened. "They know, but the risk of returning to all those star systems was too great since it was believed it would bring the Xiiginns to them. So, for the protection of the species that lived in those star systems, it was decided that the Boxans could survive by using the stasis pods until they could be retrieved after the war."

"I don't believe this. It's too long. This is too high a price," Prax'pedax said. He was unable to look away from Chazen's face on the holoscreen. He felt the fires of his rage building up inside him, and at the same time they were tinged with horrible shame that his own race had failed so completely.

"We're here now, Chazen, and I will never leave any Boxan behind. Not under my watch. Never again," Prax'pedax said.

The Boxans on the bridge came to their feet.

"Never again. These rigid protocols that leave our sisters and brothers strewn throughout the great expanse ends now. Never again!" Prax'pedax shouted, and it was repeated by the other Boxans on the bridge.

Chazen looked visibly shaken, and Prax'pedax couldn't guess at the hopelessness the Boxan must have felt during his exile.

"Thank you," Chazen said, "for myself and the rest of our kind who have yet to come home. Thank you."

Prax'pedax was tempted to send a shuttle. "We'll send a ship for you right now," he said.

"That's not necessary. I've been among Humans for a while now. They're . . . the reason I opened a comms channel is because the Humans have detected an anomaly beyond our listening station. They've detected the gravitational wave of a wormhole. At first I thought it might have been you, but it's different," Chazen said.

"Send over what you have," Prax'pedax said.

"At once, but I must also inform you that in order to get to Earth I had to break protocols and share our technology with the Humans," Chazen said.

"We're going to share a lot more with them. We'll need any advantage we can get now," Prax'pedax said and looked at his comms officer. "Tell Battle Commander Essaforn to make a sweep. I want them to investigate this anomaly. Put all ships on high alert for imminent threat of Xiiginn attack," Prax'pedax said.

"Has it come to that already?" Chazen asked.

"We're not sure, but we'll find out. I have a question for you," Prax'pedax said.

"Go ahead."

"The Humans with you now. Can you trust them?"

"I've put my life in their hands," Chazen said.

Prax'pedax nodded. He would share their technology with the Humans, but such things required a delicate touch.

"Here is one Human that I trust above all others. To him, you should listen," Chazen said.

A Human male came on screen. He had very little hair on his head, but he had a look to him that Prax'pedax was sure he'd seen in others of his kind—a sort of single-minded determination and confidence born of achievement.

"My name is Michael Hunsicker. I was the commander of the Athena before events changed that. I would urge you to contact Ed Johnson on Earth. He was part of the group that received the original warning message from your species. They've been preparing for this, and it would be a good starting point."

Prax'pedax had already met this Ed Johnson. He was one of the clever ones.

"Thank you," Prax'pedax said.

"What do you need us to do? We have a ship called the Endurance that is commanded by a man called Kyle Matthews. He's a colonel."

"I understand the military designation. I'll send a squad to your base to assess your capabilities if they'll be cleared to enter," Prax'pedax said.

"I'll make sure that happens," Michael said.

CHAPTER TWENTY-EIGHT

E dward Johnson had spent the last several days moving from place to place. The presence of the Boxans had worked as a catalyst for the countries of the world to give support to the Earth Coalition Force, or the ECF, as it had become commonly called. There was still resistance of course, but the Boxans' request to deal with one body of government capable of supporting the efforts to defend Earth in space had gotten the world's attention. The ECF was authorized to operate in space, and as a show of good faith and commitment, the spaceship Endurance was transferred to the ECF. While NASA had the most vehicles in space, it would remain a public entity in the United States of America. As of that morning, the ECF had military representation from the US, Great Britain, Canada, and the EU. Russia, China, and India had yet to formally approve—three very powerful militaries, and Ed knew that in the long run, the ECF would require the support of those nations if it was going to succeed, but they'd go to war with the army they had.

General Sheridan had been formally transferred to the ECF and would be heading it up. Details were still being agreed upon for term limits and the like, but Sheridan was in command for at least a year.

The Boxans deployed several orbital platforms that contained weapons systems of a magnitude that Humans had only dreamt about previously. The Boxans were only just beginning to disclose the platforms' capabilities, but they had disclosed that they contained a full sensor suite, along with long-range missile capabilities. The platforms were under Boxan control and managed by the team that Prax'pedax had left at the lunar base. Various military and government leaders had been outraged by this development until the first asteroids began to appear.

The asteroids heading toward the planet were not in NASA's vast database for Near-Earth Objects. At first, the appearance of multiple asteroids in the general vicinity of Earth, which Gary Hunter explained would encompass an area of several hundred million kilometers, would not have been cause for alarm, but there were too many to be a coincidence. This also put the Mars colony at risk. So far, the paths the asteroids were taking carried them past the Earth, but Ed was worried, and so was General Sheridan. The asteroids, some the size of skyscrapers, were appearing seemingly out of nowhere. During a press statement, a news blogger was attempting to bring Sheridan to task by accusing him of being an alarmist and spreading fear to consolidate power for himself and the ECF. Ed was watching the press conference on a live video feed and the camera had just focused in on General Sheridan.

"The appearance of so many of these asteroids is cause for alarm, even without the presence of the Boxans. Is it possible that these could be natural events? No, not at all. And that's not from me, but from Connie White, the director of NASA. The fact that each new asteroid we find appears closer to Earth's orbit is also cause for alarm. I believe that this could be the Xiiginns' attempt at sighting in a new weapon like you would do with a rifle—keep taking shots until the sights on your rifle line up exactly where you want them to be.

"When I took the position to head the ECF, I did so under the condition that I could be completely honest with the people of the world. We gain nothing by hiding events from the population. Anyone with a telescope can see these things. The Boxans are helping us detect them, and we'll do everything we can to keep these dangerous asteroids from reaching Earth. Either I, or someone from my staff, will provide daily updates as needed," Sheridan said.

"One more question if I may, General," the blogger asked, and Sheridan nodded for him to go on. "What can the average person do to prepare themselves?"

Sheridan gazed at the cameras. "Continue to live your lives. Trust that we're doing everything we can. More updates will follow, and advisories will be cascaded down to local law offices."

Ed switched the video feed off and sighed. Despite the unprecedented events that were taking place, the ordinary citizens were still going about their lives. There had been some minor events, but nothing like the breakdown of social services predicted by doomsday prophets. No one was in a rush to meet a dystopian world often glorified in movies and books. This could be both commendable and worrisome at the same time. Some people's desire to bury their heads in the sand could never be underestimated. When the average person looked up into the night sky, they still saw a peaceful expanse full of wonder. Ed wondered what the reaction would be if one of these asteroids actually made it to Earth. Then the panic would become all too real.

Ed watched as General Sheridan left the press release room and glanced over at him.

"I've asked the president to assign you to the ECF," Sheridan said.

Ed smirked. "Oh really, and what did she say?"

Sheridan snorted. "You're on temporary loan."

"I see," Ed said.

Sheridan glanced at the people following him. "Could you give us a minute?" he said.

Colonel Hines gave the general's followers a stern look, and they retreated.

"Walk with me," Sheridan said to Ed.

"Is Hines ECF now?" Ed asked.

"John has been with me for a while. I need to know from you whether I can trust the Boxans?" Sheridan asked.

"Why ask me?"

"At first I thought you were just an upstart spec ops contractor, but you seem to have a bead on everything that's going on. I mean to use every tool at my disposal to mitigate this threat. We don't have the means to face these Xiiginns in space, so that means this will likely become a fight that's up close and personal. The world as we know it will change overnight. I need to know if you and the resources at Dux Corp are going to back the ECF."

"We're on the same side."

"That's not an answer. Now, before you reply, I have a few things I'd like to get off my chest. I had thought that perhaps you would propose blindly trusting the Boxans once they arrived," Sheridan said.

"I don't blindly trust anyone."

Sheridan nodded. "And I bet you have contingency plans beyond count for how this is going to play out."

"You'd be correct, but I assure you I want the ECF to work. I have to ask, why the sudden change of heart?"

"In the first meeting with Prax'pedax, you asked the tough questions. I think you even took them by surprise."

"Do you think Russia, China, and India will support the ECF?" Ed asked.

Sheridan sighed. "I've spent the bulk of my career thinking of them as either the enemy or harboring enemy factions that were keen to do us harm."

"And now?"

"I'll let you know. Operating in space puts some distance between borders, as we know, but those borders will still exist up there just as they do down here."

Ed nodded.

"Back to my original question then. Can we trust the Boxans?"

"I'll give you my honest opinion. I want to say yes, but even I'm not sure. Those orbital installations under Boxan control could just as easily be pointed at us. I think it's fair to say that we just need to give them time—enough time to earn trust for their species and our own. I believe that if we can show them what we're made of, it will prove to the Boxans that Humans are a worthy ally," Ed said.

Sheridan's lips curved into a small, hard smile. "Now I know you're a believer. I wasn't sure before. Have I ever told you that I met the late great Bruce Matherson?"

Ed's eyes widened. "No, you haven't."

"Our paths crossed a couple of times."

Ed snorted. "We're here because of him."

"I need recommendations from you for staffing the ECF. I want to get the best people we have from across the globe," Sheridan said.

"I'll have Iris send you my list right away," Ed said.

Sheridan chuckled. "I should have known you'd have something like this ready. Come on. I need to brief the president and other world leaders. Oh, and one more thing. I know the Stargate program may have been canceled as a laughingstock, but ever since the Athena left Earth's orbit, we've known that it may be still alive and kicking."

Ed had been expecting this. "It is, but I need assurances for my people. They operate with a certain amount of discretion."

"We can talk about assurances. I need to know what they're capable of and how many of them there are so I can put them to good use," Sheridan said.

Ed nodded and glanced over at Iris, who, along with Colonel Hines, was watching them intently. Iris smiled, and she gave Ed a slight nod.

CHAPTER TWENTY-NINE

After the door rematerialized, Kaylan and Brenda went over every inch of the large room they were trapped in, looking for another way out. Jonah helped them search, but he seemed preoccupied with the sphere. The aqua-colored glow coming from the sphere bathed the room in a soft light. Kaylan noticed that Jonah was periodically wincing and asked Brenda to check on him.

They couldn't get out of the room. The smooth walls offered no indication that there was anything beyond the room they were in. Kaylan was reminded of standing inside the Mardoxian chamber. She glanced at the sphere, and the same message appeared that had first been displayed when they'd entered the room.

SUBMIT.

When she'd first seen it, her gut reaction had been to get as far away from the sphere as possible.

"It's an artificial intelligence, possibly the oldest one in existence," Jonah said.

He and Brenda came to Kaylan's side.

"What does it want from us?" Brenda asked.

"Perhaps it needs something from us—something it can't do for itself," Kaylan said.

"The knowledge this must contain is beyond imagining," Jonah said.

Kaylan glanced at Jonah and noticed that the left side of his face seemed to go limp. "Jonah, are you alright?"

Jonah brought his hand up to his face and touched it. "I'm not sure," he said and sank to his knees.

Brenda brought out her handheld scanner and slowly moved it from one side of his head to the other. "I don't know how he's still conscious. He's having another stroke. They're coming more frequently."

"I know," Jonah said quietly. "It's strange because I can feel it happening, but it's like there's a layer against the pain."

Kaylan looked at Brenda. "Is there anything you can do for him?"

Brenda gave her a solemn look and shook her head.

"What about on the ship?"

"On the ship I was just trying to make him as comfortable as possible," Brenda said.

Kaylan's eyes went from Brenda to Jonah.

"Kaylan, I'm fine with this," Jonah said. "I've done things . . . acted in such a way in the pursuit of knowledge . . ." He climbed back to his feet, wavering for a moment, and Brenda helped to steady him. "I never would have thought I'd be the one to have caused so much tragedy."

Kaylan swallowed hard. "The Xiiginns did this to you."

"I didn't heed Kladomaor's warning about them on Selebus. I saw one during the fighting and tried to communicate with it," Jonah said.

Kaylan's eyes widened, and she glanced at Brenda.

The sphere pulsed brightly, drawing their attention. An image appeared that showed the vast, crumbling space station.

"That's here," Brenda said.

More structures were falling, as if the lynchpins were being removed from the mega structures.

"We have to get out of here," Kaylan said.

She tried to use her senses to find the others but kept getting blocked. She glared at the sphere. "Let us out of here."

The image on the sphere disappeared, and Kaylan thought she heard a distant knocking coming from the walls.

"I think I know what it wants from us," Jonah said. He was watching the sphere with wide eyes. "And it makes a crazy kind of sense. We have to get closer to it."

"Why?" Kaylan said.

Jonah's eyes closed, and he muttered something about Zack and understanding. His head started to droop, and Kaylan helped Brenda lower him back down to the floor. Kaylan spoke Jonah's name, trying to get him to wake up.

Jonah's eyes opened. "It's a Drar artificial intelligence. Think of this place as a life boat. The AI was tasked with building it in preparation for the Drars to take up residence here, but they never came. Who knows how long this thing has been waiting here."

"Why wouldn't it repair itself?" Brenda asked.

"I don't think . . . It must have run out of resources, and during that time something miraculous happened," Jonah said.

"If you say this thing has become self-aware . . ." Brenda warned.

"There are different stages of awareness. I don't think it's like us, but there is one thing it cannot do, and we can," Jonah said.

Brenda looked questioningly at Kaylan. She raised her head and glanced back at the sphere.

"It wants us to turn it off," Kaylan said, finally understanding.

The sphere pulsed brightly, drawing their attention. The edges of the sphere pushed outward until the three of them were engulfed in the azure confines. Kaylan felt a presence in her mind. She tried to stand up but couldn't move. She started to push the presence away, fighting it. Then an image of two warring ships appeared on her internal HUD. One of the ships was Boxan, and the other was similar style to what the Xiiginns used.

Though she couldn't move, she became aware of Jonah and Brenda's presence. They were all aware of each other. Brenda seemed to rush toward Kaylan while Jonah stood apart. The Drar space station was collapsing in on itself. Images came to her mind of fleets of spaceships—huge leviathans of gray and white, each with the phoenix symbol proudly displayed on their hulls. That symbol appeared on the hull of the Athena, and Kaylan realized the Drar AI was showing her something that hadn't happened. They had no such fleet back on Earth. They didn't even know how to build ships like these yet, but here they were. Kaylan felt a sense of pride fill her at the sight of them.

The images changed to show graveyards of ships and planets from long-dead star systems. It was an image the AI had shown them before from Drar history. Then she saw the Athena. The white outer hull had become more of a shimmering silver, as if something had transformed the ship. The Athena she remembered looked clumsy in comparison to the sleek lines of the ship she was being shown.

An image of a Drar stood in front of her, and Kaylan initially flinched away, but she looked into its eyes and saw something ancient and intelligent. The Drars had the Mardoxian potential in them. They had sent spores throughout the galaxy. Many star systems passed through the forefront of her mind, too many to count. The spores that made it to life-giving planets had bestowed an evolutionary jumpstart to the species that lived there. The spores couldn't create something that wasn't already there, only nudge the potential of a species like the Drar. The spores clung to asteroids and comets and rode them through the galaxy. Some of these celestial bodies slammed into planets.

Kaylan tried to focus on who the Drars had fought. What had led such an advanced alien race to their destruction? Was it some unseen enemy, or something else? She felt that the knowledge was there but was being withheld, as if the AI was deciding what was most important to share. Kaylan stopped pushing for knowledge, her own instincts at once giving light to the many paths they could take, and she searched for the one that didn't end with all of them dying. The Boxans sought control as galactic gardeners. The Xiiginns sought to dominate and conquer and exploit the universe. What role would humanity take? What would they do if they survived to explore the galaxy? As the questions tumbled through her mind, she saw different outcomes, perceiving bits of humanity in each of the alien species they'd encountered. There had to be a balance —a balance that would allow life to flourish and at the same time prevent a species like the Xiiginns from taking over the galaxy.

The azure curtain passed from Kaylan and she could move again. She heard Brenda gasp and looked over at her. Jonah Redford was walking inside the sphere. Kaylan called out to him, and Jonah cocked his head to the side as if he hadn't quite heard her.

Kaylan and Brenda stood up, looking at each other in alarm. A doorway on the far side of the room dematerialized. Kaylan and Brenda circled around, calling out to Jonah. They came around to where Jonah was standing and saw his wide-eyed gaze. He finally seemed to notice them.

"You have to get out of there," Kaylan said.

She stepped toward the semitransparent sphere, but Brenda gripped her arm, prepared to pull Kaylan back.

Jonah's mouth was moving, but Kaylan couldn't hear what he was saying. The sphere was getting smaller. Kaylan reached out and touched the sphere.

"It's okay," Redford was saying. "I was never walking out of here."

"We can help you. We can get you to Kladomaor's ship and . . ."

Redford shook his head. "There's too much damage," Redford said. He looked over at Brenda. "Thank you for trying. You never gave up, and I want you to know how much I appreciate it."

"How do you know we can't help you? This place has helped you. There has to be something we can do," Kaylan said.

Redford frowned, and his eyes grew distant, as if he were in two places at once. "Tell Zack he was right. You need to leave.

Once I power down this place, it will collapse on itself and unleash all the remaining energy."

Brenda pulled Kaylan back. "Come on. It's what he wants," she said.

Kaylan let herself be pulled back. The azure glow around the sphere intensified until they could no longer see Jonah Redford, and then it was gone. The room went dark.

Brenda pulled her beyond the door, and it rematerialized as soon as they were beyond the threshold.

CHAPTER THIRTY

The bridge of the Boxan ship was eerily silent. They'd been waiting for the Xiiginn scout ship to make its move. Kladomaor had gone over different scenarios in his mind, trying to find an outcome that prevented the Xiiginns from gaining access to the Drar space station. He kept his ship's position between the Xiiginn scout ship and the space station. During their blockade, they had moved beyond the point in space where the space station had originally opened fire on him, but now it didn't. The Drars must have surmised what Kladomaor intended.

He glanced at Ma'jasalax. Her only advice had been to give the Athena as much time as possible, so that's what he was doing. They couldn't go into stealth mode, which severely limited their capabilities as a warship. The stealth ship's design wasn't one of heavy armor plating, its strength being to sneak up on the enemy. Their ship did have large graser cannons, which were more powerful than point-defense laser cannons. The graser cannons were mounted forward and aft, meant to overwhelm the enemy using a powerful laser blast. They couldn't be maintained for long, however, so timing their shots was critical to extracting the highest price from their enemy's ship. Unfortunately, they had no missiles left in their armory. He could have used some long-range fusion warheads that could easily ruin a Xiiginn scout ship's day. Besides grasers, they had rail cannon capable of firing kinetic payloads, but again, he was limited to a short distance. There was simply no way he could face the Xiiginn scout ship and come away without taking damage to his own ship.

Xiiginn scout ships weren't designed for a standup conflict. They were meant for firing a few shots and then using their superior speed to get themselves to freedom.

"What can we do?" Gaarokk asked.

Kladomaor blew out a determined breath. "The fact of the matter is they can outmaneuver us, and they have longer-range weapons. So we take the fight head-on—convince them we're making our final all-out attack run."

Gaarokk glanced nervously at Ma'jasalax. "Won't that get us all killed?"

"If we stay here and wait for them to pick us off, we will most certainly die," Kladomaor said. The other Boxans on the bridge were watching him, waiting for him to give the command that would commit them to a course of action they might not fly away from.

"Battle stations," Kladomaor ordered. "Start active scans. I want a missile lock on their ship."

"We're locked, Battle Commander," Triflan said.

"All ahead full for ten micro-cycles," Kladomaor ordered.

Their ship sped forward with a sudden burst. The Xiiginn scout ship came about.

"They've fired two . . . make that four missiles," Triflan said.

"More speed," Kladomaor ordered. "Point missile defense online. Ready grasers to fire on the enemy ship when it gets in range."

The Boxan ship barreled forward into the Xiiginn missiles. Only four. The commander of the scout ship didn't know Kladomaor didn't have any missiles of his own. The Xiiginn commander assumed, because of the missile lock, that Kladomaor was moments from firing his arsenal. It was a bluff, and each moment carried him closer to his target—closer to taking out those evil galactic parasites. He *was* his ship, his crew, and its weapons. The ship was his body, the crew was his hands, and the weapons were his fury.

"Evasive maneuvers. Launch countermeasures at once," Kladomaor said.

The Boxan ship had darted forward, intent on closing the distance to the scout ship. Countermeasures fired ahead and veered away, drawing the incoming missiles with them. Varek angled the ship back toward the scout ship.

"Fire," Kladomaor said.

The Xiiginn scout ship fired more missiles, but the molten fury of the blast from the stealth ship's grasers tore through them before they could arm.

"Direct hit. We've damaged their forward missile tubes," Triflan said.

"Fire the rail cannon and keep firing until we pass them. I want that ship full of holes before we're done," Kladomaor said.

The lighting on the bridge dimmed with each shot from rail cannon, and Kladomaor saw that Engineering had diverted auxiliary power to the weapons systems. The damage they were doing now was the best they were going to be able to do.

Alarms on the bridge blared all at once as the Xiiginns finally fired their close-range weapons, tearing into his already damaged ship. Kladomaor had the combat output on screen from the warfare AI. Multiple hull breaches were being detected throughout the ship. His soldiers were dying. The rail cannon went offline. Damage to the forward section of the ship had taken out their grasers.

"Bring us down point nine zero, now!" Kladomaor said.

Once Varek confirmed the order, Kladomaor ordered the aft grasers to keep firing until they couldn't fire anymore.

The two ships tore into one another, venting atmosphere and lives into space. The two warring races continued to fire their weapons until at last the distance made further firing of their weapons ineffective.

"Damage report," Kladomaor said.

Half the systems were down on the bridge. Emergency lighting had cut over as auxiliary power was diverted to life support.

"We've lost main engines one and three, and we don't have lateral control. Remaining weapons systems are overloaded," Triflan said.

"When can the main engines be restored?" Kladomaor asked.

"They can't, Battle Commander. Main engines one and three are completely destroyed. Main engine two is at thirty percent power and is the only reason we're still moving at all," Triflan said.

"What's the status of the Xiiginns?" Kladomaor asked.

"They're not pursuing. I'm not sure they can. They're pretty banged up, just like we are, Battle Commander," Varek said.

Kladomaor used his neural implants and cycled through the reports. The Cherubian drive was still intact, but without main power they couldn't open a wormhole.

"Tell Engineering to get me main power back," Kladomaor said.

"No response from Engineering," Triflan said, and a hush swept over the bridge.

"Acknowledged," Kladomaor said.

A comms channel opened to the bridge. "This is Etanu, Battle Commander. I'm heading to Engineering. I will report in when I get there."

Kladomaor's brows rose, and Ma'jasalax gave him a knowing look. "Acknowledged, Etanu, and thank you."

"We're still in this fight, Battle Commander. I'll get the power restored," Etanu said.

Kladomaor felt the edges of his lips lift, but it was gone in an instant. "Tactical, I want eyes on the Xiiginns at all times. You have operational authority to fire whatever we have at them should they decide to make another pass at us."

There was a soft rumbling from the Boxans on the bridge—low at first but gaining in intensity. Kladomaor found that he was swept up along with it. He glanced at Ma'jasalax and found that she sang along with Gaarokk. They were all soldiers now, and their battle song was not yet over. These waves would ride through the great expanse. Let the Xiiginns fear the wrath of the Boxans. This fight was far from over.

CHAPTER THIRTY-ONE

Time was always against them. Prax'pedax had only been in this star system for a short while and already he felt that time was growing short. They'd deployed a number of orbital platforms meant to bolster Earth's defenses. He'd also deployed two engineering platforms to jumpstart the advanced tech base they needed to establish here. A team of Boxans was sent to the Human lunar base to oversee the new systems. If there'd been more time, he would have done more.

"Essaforn is overdue," Thesulia said.

Prax'pedax swung his gaze toward the Mardoxian priestess. Essaforn was the commander of the Dreadnaught ship he'd sent to investigate the anomalous wormhole activity. He'd been so preoccupied with investigating the source of the asteroids suddenly appearing within the vicinity of the Human home world that he'd overlooked Essaforn's mission.

"Open a comms channel to the ECF base on the moon," Prax'pedax said.

After a few moments, Chazen's face appeared on the main holoscreen.

"Battle Leader," Chazen said.

"Who is the ranking ECF official on base?" Prax'pedax said.

"Commander Alissa Archer is in charge of this base," Chazen said.

"Patch her in," Prax'pedax said.

A Human female joined Chazen on screen.

"Commander, I'm turning over the orbital defense system to you. In a moment, I'll transfer authorization and protocols to my team there, and they will be under your command," Prax'pedax said.

"Where are you going?" Commander Archer asked.

"The ship I sent to investigate the area you call the Oort Cloud is long overdue. It is our belief that the Xiiginns are here but for some reason haven't made their presence known. We go on the hunt," Prax'pedax said.

He watched as the base commander thought about her next question, but she didn't ask it. Instead her expression became one of regret and hardened determination. "Good luck to you. We hope you find your missing ship."

Prax'pedax cut the comms channel and glanced at Thesulia. The orbital platforms would help aid Earth's defenses, but they were intended to be a backup defensive strategy and not a primary means of defense. The main holoscreen showed the position of all the spacecraft in the area. He noted that the Human ship with the designation Endurance flew at the Lagrange point between the Earth and the sun.

Prax'pedax opened a comms channel to the third Dreadnaught, and within moments Battle Commander Vuloyant was onscreen.

"I've been expecting your comms channel, Battle Leader," Vuloyant said.

"Best speed out. We'll stagger our approach," Prax'pedax said.

"Wouldn't it be prudent that you wait behind while I take my ship to investigate?" Vuloyant asked.

Prax'pedax shook his head. "We're stronger together. We'll find out what fighting force the Xiiginns have brought here."

"Battle Leader, I must log my protest. Our mandate is to lend protection to this star system. This can be achieved by staging our operations beyond the asteroid belt."

"My orders stand, Battle Commander."

Battle Commander Vuloyant snapped a salute to Prax'pedax, and the comms channel was switched off.

Vuloyant wasn't being insubordinate; it was a commander's duty to point out a differing way to achieve an objective. What would have been insubordinate was if Vuloyant had insisted on his standpoint after Prax'pedax had given an actual order. Perhaps Kladomaor's ways of doing things was having an influential effect on him. Conventionally, they were losing their war with the Xiiginns. Slowly but decisively, they'd been pushed back on all fronts.

Prax'pedax gave the order for them to deploy. Their heading was the last known trajectory of their lost Dreadnaught. The massive Boxan ship was capable of fighting off a standard Xiiginn warship battle group, and Battle Commander Essaforn should have been able to send a communication back to him if he'd encountered the Xiiginns. Intelligence and enemy locations were worth more at times than engaging the enemy. He didn't want to think about whether Essaforn had been taken by surprise. The Boxan Dreadnaught was superior to a Xiiginn warship in armament and sheer power. As they raced across the star system, Prax'pedax wondered what had happened to their wayward ship.

"Active scans. I want an accurate picture of the area just outside the ninth orbital body," Prax'pedax said.

Active scans would give away their position, but ships of the wall weren't meant to fight from the shadows, and at this range, a battle was won by positioning the pieces on the battlefield.

While they raced to the outer fringes of the star system, his mind wandered back to his interactions with the Humans. Turning over the orbital defense platforms to Human control was in direct violation of military protocols from the High Council. He'd given orders to the team left behind to educate the Humans on the engineering platforms after the defense platforms were fully operational. Prax'pedax supposed that if they made it back to the colony, he could explain his actions by arguing the efficient use of resources, and the Humans were a resource in this equation. Understandably, they were eager to defend their planet from the threat of an invasion force. Having perused the data on Human history collected by the listening post, he'd learned that Humans were no strangers to war. Conflict had a way of forging intelligent species, with the question always being whether they would eventually abandon their barbaric ways or embrace them to their own detriment.

The Boxans had chosen a peaceful path until the Xiiginns had betrayed them. When conflict with the Xiiginns became a matter of Boxan survival, they'd been forced to embrace their primal instincts. The fate of his species demanded that he become a protector. He saw the same strength in the Humans, and he was finding that he wanted to speak to more of them. They were primitive in many ways, with an economic system that was decidedly reversed, but there was a rich cultural heritage revealed in many practices all over their planet. The many faces of humanity were at once beautiful and terrifying in their vast potential.

There had been a small group of ECF soldiers and scientists aboard their ship, but he'd had to cut his time with them short. Once the asteroids started to appear, he knew he would be taking his ship into a conflict that might be the end of them all, but the Human leader had been adamant about staying with them. They had a pressing need to make themselves useful, so Prax'pedax had reluctantly allowed a small group to stay aboard. They would be watched over by his crew. Prax'pedax had found that the true measure of any species could be found on the battlefield. It was decidedly un-Boxan of him to have these thoughts, but the many cycles of battles over the course of this long war had changed him.

"You're very quiet," Thesulia said.

"I was just thinking that I would have liked more time with the Humans," Prax'pedax said.

"They are an interesting species with massive potential. I was glad to see that Ma'jasalax hadn't overstated this."

"Do you mean to say that the Mardoxian sect isn't unified in its approach to guiding the rest of the Boxans along?"

Thesulia regarded him for a moment but didn't answer.

"The Humans have no idea of what they'll face, and in the

face of the great mystery, they'll throw themselves against it to protect their home," Prax'pedax said.

"They share a lot with the Nershals in that respect."

"Perhaps with a little less pride than the Nershals exhibit," Prax'pedax said.

He glanced at the main holodisplay and noted Vuloyant's position. During their journey, he'd broken off to approach from a different vector. Both ships would have active sensors sweeping the area.

"Battle Leader, we've detected Commander Essaforn's ship," Wynog said.

The main holodisplay changed to that of a heaping wreck that had once been a Boxan Dreadnaught. The massive hull had been chewed up, and there were large gashes on the battle-steel hull.

The scanners were already tracking for lifesigns or escape pods in the area. The structure where the main engines should have been had been fully destroyed.

"Are there any other ships in the area?" Prax'pedax asked.

"Nothing," Wynog replied.

"Send word to Vuloyant that we're not alone out here and to prepare for imminent attack. We'll join up in section five," Prax'pedax said.

His comms officer confirmed that the message had been sent.

"Contact," Wynog said. "Multiple contacts, Battle Leader."

Prax'pedax switched the view on the main holodisplay to show a tactical readout. His eyes widened at the number of Xiiginn contacts at the edge of scanner range. Prax'pedax waited as the electronic warfare AI went to work, classifying each enemy target and highlighting the known capabilities. The Xiiginns had sent a massive force to this star system. Prax'pedax knew Vuloyant would see the same thing, if he hadn't already.

"We'll make our stand here. Deploy long-range missile platforms and send a comms buoy back to command central with this message: Alpha. Alpha. Alpha. End transmission," Prax'pedax said.

The bridge officers went to work. Command central at their colony would be informed, but they would be in no position to send help in time. He continued to give out orders leveraging everything at his disposal.

"Ready our strike-fighter squadrons one through five. I want all our ships in the air. The Xiiginns expect us to be cowed by an overwhelming force. Let's give them a fight to remember—one for their very lives. The people of Earth are depending on us. The Boxans have answered the call, and the Xiiginns will hear our battle song before we're extinguished from the great expanse."

He used his neural link to send an encrypted command down to the shuttle bays where he'd sent the group of Humans who hadn't wanted to be left behind. The shuttles would get them back to Earth, along with members of his crew he'd preselected. He fully expected the Humans not to cooperate and had authorized the use of stunners.

He glanced at Thesulia and her bodyguard. Kray watched him and waited.

"I'll stand with you, Battle Leader," Thesulia said.

"I can't guarantee your safety. You'd better serve by returning to Earth to guide the Humans," Prax'pedax said.

Thesulia tucked in her chin and gave him a stubborn look.

"My place is here. I'll use my gifts to help you, and should the Xiiginns win this battle, Kray will fulfill his duty."

Thesulia didn't wait for his answer, focusing her attention on the tactical screen, and Prax'pedax turned his attention to the battle about to be fought. The Mardoxian priestess would insert her feedback into his tactics, and they would fight together.

CHAPTER THIRTY-TWO

Ed Johnson authorized encrypted communication protocols to two of his covert operation centers. These were hidden Dux Corp facilities that had been utilized in intelligence-gathering, but now they were being used to help them identify incoming asteroids. General Sheridan had been insistent that these people be moved to a designated ECF facility, but Ed had refused. Not only would it be a massive waste of time when they needed to utilize any intelligence resource they could muster, but they were officially not part of the ECF at this time.

General Sheridan didn't like it, but he couldn't make a compelling argument when they had so many other things to worry about. The ECF had been coordinating with militaries around the globe, including those who hadn't officially joined.

Iris pressed her hand on Ed's shoulder. "Incoming message from home office," she said.

Ed transferred his clearance code in addition to his DNA

authentication, saw the message, and immediately sent it over to Sheridan's staff.

"Priority one," Ed announced.

Colonel Hines acknowledged and processed it as best he could. They'd have to come up with a better way to communicate, but they were putting this new organization together on the fly.

"Is this accurate?" Sheridan asked, glancing over from his work area.

"My people can just point us in the right direction. They can't give precise measurements other than saying it's big or really big, as the analyst has indicated. The Endurance is in the area. Have them confirm," Ed said.

Orders were relayed to the Endurance. Their communications capabilities had drastically sped up since they'd reverse engineered the Boxan comms array that Chazen had initially sent them several months ago. Coincidentally, it had been good practice, giving engineers across the globe a rudimentary foundation in one slice of Boxan technology. Prax'pedax had seemed impressed that they were able to reverse engineer it at all.

"General, I have an alpha priority message directly to you from Prax'pedax," Colonel Hines said.

Sheridan stepped away from the people around him and used his PDA to retrieve the message. Ed stopped what he was doing and watched as Sheridan let out a great sigh and waved him over.

"The Boxans have engaged the Xiiginns out in the Oort Cloud," Sheridan said. "Listen up, people," the general barked.

He used his PDA to transfer the message out to their screens. Ed watched as Prax'pedax told them what they'd discovered and that they were about to engage the enemy. Ed had never felt so powerless. There was nothing any of them could do, and a profound silence descended upon those in the room.

"They're fighting for us to give us as much time as they can so we can prepare ourselves. Let's not waste it. I want this message transferred to every nation's leader right now. Advise them to put all militaries on high alert. I want the Boxans stationed at the lunar base to give us estimates on how long it would take a Xiiginn warship to reach Earth. Let's run the numbers and have plans ready to set in motion," Sheridan said.

The stunned silence evaporated in an instant as the newly formed ECF personnel went to work. Inaction and a lack of preparedness was the key to defeat. They didn't have what they needed to fight the Xiiginns in space for very long, but they wouldn't simply allow them to land on their planet without a fight.

"Comms request from the Endurance," Gary Hunter said from his console.

"Go ahead. Put it on the main wall screen," Sheridan said.

". . . a massive asteroid over fourteen hundred miles in diameter, and it's heading directly toward the Earth," Colonel Kyle Matthews said.

There were gasps from those in the command center.

"That's more than half the size of the moon," Gary Hunter said.

Ed's mouth hung open. The Xiiginns had somehow sent a massive celestial body toward the Earth.

"I thought the Xiiginns would send an invasion force, not something that would take out the whole damn planet," Sheridan said.

Ed didn't know what to say. He simply couldn't wrap his brain around something that large heading directly for Earth.

"I need ideas, people. Call anyone you have to. Focus on solutions," Sheridan said.

Another comms channel was open from the lunar base, and Chazen's wide head appeared on screen.

"We've just received word from the Endurance," Chazen said.

"Please tell us the orbital defense platforms have something that can destroy this thing," Sheridan said.

Chazen's large brows pushed forward. "Defense platforms are meant for engaging ships, not destroying moon-sized asteroids."

Sheridan glanced around the room. "There has to be something we can do. Anything?" he said.

A creepy silence took hold of everyone. This was just something none of them were equipped to deal with.

"General, I think you should take a look at this," the comms officer said.

A video broadcast came on the main wall screen. It showed a humanoid being with platinum-colored hair and dark violet eyes. Its features were strikingly Human and alien at the same time.

"Citizens of Earth. I am Garm Antis of the Xiiginn Empire. We are representatives of the Confederation of Species sent to your star system on a diplomatic mission."

"I want that signal isolated," Sheridan said.

"You've been misinformed by the Boxans. They've told you we've been using our technology to hurl asteroids at your planet, and I'm here to tell you that this is a Boxan lie. We've only just arrived at the outer fringes of your star system and were immediately engaged by a Boxan Dreadnaught ship. We observed them using their Cherubian drives to open a wormhole. That wormhole was in the path of the asteroids," Garm Antis said.

"Signal locked, General," an intelligence analyst said.

"How do we know you're telling the truth?" Sheridan asked.

Garm Antis's brows drew up in surprise, but he quickly covered it up. "I'm delighted to speak to a Human for the first time. To whom am I speaking?"

"I'm General William Sheridan of the Earth Coalition Force."

"I'm very pleased to make your acquaintance," Garm Antis said.

"If you want to show us good faith, stop hurling asteroids toward our planet," Sheridan said.

"Sir," Colonel Hines said softly. "The president wishes to speak with you."

Sheridan gave Hines a shallow nod but remained focused on the Xiiginn.

"As I've said, we caught the Boxans—"

"I'm not the first Human your species has been in contact with. We've had reports that you took a member of the Athena and held him prisoner. How would you care to explain those actions?"

"I'm afraid I'm not sure what you're talking about," Garm Antis said. The Xiiginn's pale skin became darker.

"His name is Zack Quick. He was held at one of your facilities on a planet called Selebus in the Nerva star system. Are there any more lies you'd like to spout before I cut the connection?" Sheridan asked.

Garm Antis glanced at something off-screen, and the broadcast was cut off.

"Can we block that signal?" Sheridan asked.

"We can," Ed said. "Let me make a few calls."

Colonel Hines cleared his throat.

"Put her on screen," Sheridan said.

"General Sheridan, you were not authorized to speak with that alien on humanity's behalf," Halloway said.

"Madam President, you gave me a job to protect the Earth from extraterrestrial threats, and that Xiiginn represents a clear threat to the Earth," Sheridan said.

President Halloway took a steadying breath. "You could have negotiated a ceasefire and bought us some time."

"I will not allow an occupying force to land unopposed. I'm authorized to act in defense of the Earth, not only by the United States but by a long list of other countries around the world," Sheridan said.

President Halloway looked taken aback for a moment and then realized that this was an argument she couldn't win. "Carry on, General. My office will be in touch."

The call ended, and Ed came to Sheridan's side.

"I have to admit I didn't think you'd openly defy the president," Ed said.

Sheridan loosened his collar. "Neither did I," he said.

"Why the sudden change of heart?" Ed asked.

"It happened when that alien came on screen. Discord is their weapon. They'll enamor us with pretty speeches while they squeeze the life out of us. The ECF will likely fire me the moment they get the chance," Sheridan said.

"Not for one year, at least," Ed said.

"Excuse me," Gary Hunter said. "I had an idea about the large asteroid heading toward Earth. I don't think we can stop it,

206 | KEN LOZITO

but there might be a way to keep it from killing us . . . at least immediately. I'll need to confer with some friends at Mission Control."

"Let's hear what you've got, son," Sheridan said.

Gary Hunter laid out a high-level plan to deal with an asteroid half the size of the moon. Nothing they had could deal with it directly. Ed listened as Gary put forth hopeful assumptions that the Boxans had certain components at their disposal. Ed supposed a shot in the dark was better than nothing. It would have to be.

CHAPTER THIRTY-THREE

Kaylan stood outside the room, staring at the door that had rematerialized moments before. Brenda was gasping.

"He just disappeared. Jonah is gone!" Brenda said.

Kaylan focused, and she was able to see into the other room. It was all dark and empty. Wherever Jonah had gone, he was no longer in that room. "We have to find the others. There isn't much time," Kaylan said.

She had to pull Brenda away from the large door.

"He's not in there anymore," Kaylan said.

Brenda turned toward her, and they began walking. "Where did he go?"

"You heard him. He was dying. He said he was going to give us as much time as he could before this place . . ." Kaylan's voice trailed off.

Brenda swallowed hard and blew out a breath. "Let's go," she said.

They continued on and before long their strides had lengthened until they were moving at a slow jog. Kaylan tried to reach Zack on her PDA, but there was no reply. They stopped at the end of a corridor that split in two directions, and she thought she heard someone yelling. Kaylan and Brenda sprinted down the left corridor until it came to a large atrium. The remaining crew of the Athena was clustered there.

Kaylan cried out to them, and they all went instantly silent. Zack recovered first and ran toward her, pulling her into a quick embrace.

"How did you get free? We couldn't get through the door, and we were looking for another way inside," Zack said.

"Where's Jonah?" Hicks asked.

"He's gone," Kaylan said.

Zack glanced from Kaylan to Brenda. "What do you mean, he's gone? Is he trapped?"

"No," Kaylan said and proceeded to tell them what happened to Redford.

Brenda went over to Zack. "He said to tell you that you were right. That you'd understand what he had to do."

Zack rubbed his eyes and ran his fingers down his face. "It's the AI. That has to be it."

"I cannot account for Dr. Redford's behavior," the Athena's AI said. Her voice was coming through the speakers inside their helmets.

"You're back online! Oh, thank god," Zack said.

"Athena, transmit your current coordinates. We have to get out of here," Kaylan said.

"At once, Commander. Trans . . . Oh, *that's* different," the AI said.

Kaylan glanced at Zack. "Athena, we need those coordinates," she said.

A second later the coordinates to the Athena appeared on their individual HUDs.

"I'm afraid I cannot reach Dr. Redford's suit computer. It's currently offline."

"Understood. We're on our way," Kaylan said.

They started moving out. "The AI seemed different, like it was uncertain," Hicks said.

"We'll find out when we get there," Kaylan said.

"What were you going to say?" Hicks asked Zack.

Zack was frowning, and it looked like he was working within his own internal HUD while trying to keep from tripping over anyone.

"Right," Zack said. "The Drars built their own artificial intelligence into this place."

"Like the Boxans," Hicks said.

Zack glanced around them. They were passing a set of windows that showed the crumbling landscape of an ancient city.

"Probably not like the Boxans, but think of it like this: The AI, us, and the Drars all operate within a set of rules. The AI that built this place is beyond anything we've ever come across," Zack said.

"Seems like a waste to bring us all the way out here when it just needs someone to turn the damn thing off," Hicks said.

"There was more to it than that," Kaylan said. "It seemed to be trying to decide something about us in particular."

"We still don't know why it took our ship," Hicks said.

They rounded the corner, and a large door dematerialized in front of them. There was a long, wide path, and the Athena hovered at the end of it. The crew came to a stop. There were thousands of drones swarming the ship, but it hardly looked like the ship Kaylan remembered. The Drar AI hadn't lied to them. The images it had shown them had been real.

"It looks like they fixed it up," Zack said.

The ground beneath their feet started to shake, causing some of them to lose their balance. Hicks urged them toward the Athena.

"How are we going to fly the ship if we don't know what's been done to it?" Zack asked.

Kaylan was still taking it in. The sleek lines of the hull seemed more refined. Even the shuttle gleamed as if it were brand new. The Lenoy Salvage System was simply gone, and in its place was a protrusion that was part of the hull.

"Someone is accessing my suit computer," Zack said. "And my implants. What the . . ."

Kaylan felt it too. There was a slight buzzing in the back of her mind, intense enough to make her aware that it was there but not enough to distract her entirely.

The rest of the crew had similar sensations. A platform rose several inches from the ground and they climbed on top of it. Kaylan glanced around at the massive alien space station. She could have spent a lifetime here learning all its secrets. If this was just some kind of remnant Drar installation, what had become of them? Where had they gone? Why had the Drar AI decided to help them? Her mind kept spitting out questions with no answers.

The platform rose into the air. Buildings were crumbling all around them as far as they could see. The thousands of drones that had been swarming their ship were beginning to fall away, as if their job was done and they were no longer needed. The platform brought them to the airlock doors, which opened at their approach. The inner airlock was much larger than it had been before. They could all get inside, and once the last person had stepped off the platform, it fell away, disintegrating into nothing. The outer door shut, and jets of air were pumped into the room. Then the inner doors opened. The room beyond looked the same, with spots for all of them to put their EVA suits now that they were no longer needed.

"Athena, begin prep of the main engines," Kaylan said. "Efren and Nikolai, I need you guys to do a full diagnostic of the major systems as quickly as you can. We need to leave this place in a hurry."

"Commander, what if they've changed the internal components? I can't guarantee the diagnostics will work properly," Efren said.

Kaylan finished removing her EVA suit. "I know. Just do the best you can . . . Do you guys still feel that buzzing?" she asked.

Zack and the others nodded.

Curious, but Kaylan had to push those thoughts aside. They needed to know if the Athena was flight-ready.

"Katie and Vitomir, I need you to check the engine systems. Brenda and Emma, I need you to check the auxiliary systems, including life support. Zack and Hicks, you're with me on the bridge," Kaylan said.

Beyond the EVA prep room, the rest of the ship looked different. Instead of multiple compartments lining the walls down each of the corridors, the walls were smooth. There were panels outside every door, but they looked to be more a part of the surface than before. The three of them walked slowly, taking in all the differences.

"It's like it has that new-car smell," Zack said. "Athena, can you give us a report on what's been changed?"

"Of course, but that would impinge on efficiency, making our probability of leaving this Drar facility—"

"You could just say not now, and that would be fine," Zack said.

"Confirmed," the AI said. "I've opened up a data feed to each of your implants, as well as upgraded the brain implant interface."

Zack glanced at Kaylan in alarm.

"Athena, we talked about upgrades. They're not to be done without our permission," Zack said.

"Those were the existing parameters, but the systems and internal components have changed, including my capabilities. My operating instructions included that the first thing I was to do upon the crew's return was upload this information," the AI said.

"It's alright," Kaylan said. "I don't think all this would have been done if it was going to hurt us."

"Yeah, but now we can hurt ourselves because we don't know what we're doing," Zack said.

"Let's get to the bridge," Kaylan said.

As they made their way through the ship, more things looked different, but they couldn't take the time to explore right now.

"Holy crap!" Zack said. "They completely upgraded the ship's computing systems."

They came to the door of the bridge, and it opened the same as before. The large conference table with holodisplay, comms station, and commander's station near the front were still there. It looked as if they had changed everything but kept the ship's configuration familiar enough that they could still fly it.

"The storage capacity is above and beyond anything I've ever seen. I don't even know how this all works . . . Wait a minute," Zack said. He was frowning at the console. "I see it now. Updated ship protocols and procedures are there for the picking."

Kaylan went over to the commander's chair, with Hicks climbing into the pilot's seat.

The ship's holo-interface came online, and she brought up the emergency startup procedures.

"Engines are online," Hicks said. "Efren is reporting similar things to what Zack is seeing—expanded power output across all systems."

A private comms channel opened up to Kaylan. It was coming from Jonah's EVA suit outside the ship.

"Get our people home, Commander," Jonah said.

His voice sounded as if he were speaking from a vast, echoing chamber.

A countdown timer appeared on her HUD, and the comms channel closed before Kaylan could reply. The navigation computer put up a course for them to take. The buzzing in the back of her head finally stopped, and a working knowledge of the interface seemed to bubble up to the surface. Kaylan's mouth hung open.

Hicks looked over at her and frowned. "What is it?"

"Bring up the navigation interface and tell me what you see," Kaylan said.

Hicks did as he was asked, and his eyes widened at the options on the holoscreen. A wide smile spread across his face.

"We're going to get out of here," Hicks said.

"Damn right we are," Kaylan said. She engaged the ship-wide broadcast. "Find your seats, ladies and gentlemen. We're leaving."

Kaylan did a last-minute check of systems status, and they were green across the board, even the new systems she hadn't had time to fully explore yet.

"Kaylan," Zack said, "the sensors are showing severe degradation from the perimeter of the shroud."

"Time for us to leave," Kaylan said and engaged the Athena's engines.

CHAPTER THIRTY-FOUR

In the fringes of the great expanse, two ships engaged in battle, both leaking atmosphere from hundreds of hull breaches. Earlier, Kladomaor had ordered all their passengers to go to individual life support. They'd continued to trade blows with the Xiiginn scout ship while they could but had stopped for the moment. Both ships were severely damaged. His crew were putting everything they had into keeping the ship combat-ready, but it wasn't enough. The only weapon they had left was the ship itself. Their graser cannons were offline and were likely never to come back online again. They had lost two of their main engines, and the third couldn't safely give them anything above thirty percent capacity. Auxiliary systems were virtually nonexistent. He couldn't even turn the ship around and ram the Xiiginn scout ship if he wanted to.

"Battle Commander, sensors continue to report that the distortion field is reducing. The Drar space station will fully emerge into the great expanse within three micro-cycles," Triflan said.

Kladomaor glanced up at the main holodisplay out of habit, but it wasn't working anymore. He switched to his own console. "Varek, have you been able to raise the Athena on comms?"

"Negative, Battle Commander. I'll keep trying," Varek said.

During the battle with the Xiiginn scout ship, he'd drawn them in, hoping the Drar defense systems would damage the scout ship, but nothing had happened, and he couldn't decide whether that was a good thing or a bad thing. Kladomaor glanced at Ma'jasalax and was reluctant to say what she already knew. They were about to die. This battle was to be their last. Kladomaor couldn't hold with the irony that a cruel twist of fate was preventing him from making one last run at the Xiiginns. Instead, he was stuck going in one direction.

"Battle Commander," Etanu's voice came over comms. "We can't get the Cherubian drive back online. The bypass from main engines one and three has failed. There's simply too much damage. Maybe if we had a week . . ."

"Understood. Stand by," Kladomaor said.

There was nothing he could do now but wait for the inevitable. The Xiiginns would fix their weapons systems and destroy his ship. Kladomaor had exacted a heavy toll from the Xiiginns, but it wasn't enough.

"Battle Commander, I'm picking up a gravitational anomaly from within the Drar space station," Triflan said.

Kladomaor was about to order it on the main holoscreen, but stopped himself. He kept forgetting it was no longer there.

Ma'jasalax came to his side.

"These readings show that the shroud field is dissipating," Kladomaor said.

He glanced over at Triflan, and the Boxan shook his head. No word from the Athena. What had happened to the Humans?

"Battle Commander, the Xiiginns are increasing their speed and will soon close in on our position," Triflan said.

Kladomaor acknowledged the status update. This was it. There was nothing he could do. Their ship was barely holding together as it was.

"The anomaly is getting stronger," Triflan said.

Kladomaor brought the data feeds to his console.

CHAPTER THIRTY-FIVE

T he area of the great expanse the Humans called the Oort
Cloud was home to icy debris that was left over from
when this star system had formed. Prax'pedax had noted that
there were vast resources here, and had there been time, the
Humans would probably have used these resources to build ships
of their own. But their battle with the Xiiginn fleet was
disrupting the harmony of the objects here that had taken
millions of cycles to create. Missiles tipped with fusion warheads
gouged into the Xiiginn fleet, disabling or destroying many of
their ships. The Boxan Dreadnaughts were ships of the wall,
capable of dealing out immeasurable damage, but at the end of a
cycle it came down to a numbers game, and the Xiiginn battle
leader knew it. Prax'pedax knew they could only fire so many
missiles. Their squadrons of strike-fighters were almost depleted,
and yet none had asked to retreat. The strike-fighter pilots fought
and would die here, taking as many of the Xiiginns with them as

they could. This was their commitment to the Human race—a young species with massive potential.

If he'd held with the strict Boxan stance on a species like the Humans, they would have waited a few hundred more cycles to determine whether they would be granted access to the Confederation. A few hundred more cycles would have given the Humans time to mature or wipe themselves out. It seemed to be the inherent danger of intelligent species that they were the arbiters of their own destruction, but that was not the case here. The Boxans couldn't allow that to happen. In addition to their Mardoxian potential, the Humans had a number of things going for them to make them prime candidates as allies: numbers, for one. There were so many of them. Second was their great capacity for compassion and loyalty, which was balanced with conflicts and violence. In all the species the Boxans had observed, there was a constant truth present. In order to rise as an intelligent species, they had to endure a period of time when they must face the horrors of war. They must face the great evil and the power that comes from conflict and then turn away from it. They must learn that harmony cannot be achieved without first facing the evil that can stem from themselves.

The Boxans had endured it and then later had to return to those ways. It was a bitter cycle, but it was also the price of survival. The cycle of conflict was with them and was something the Xiiginns had embraced. The Xiiginns had taken control of the Confederation from them, but that wasn't the reason the Boxans fought. They fought because they had put the Xiiginns on this path of galactic conquest, and it was only now that they were starting to accept that they could not stop the Xiiginns alone.

Their first attempt had been to seek out species that could resist the Xiiginn influence. They'd believed the Nershals could fill this void, and though they *could* directly resist Xiiginn compulsion, the Boxans had learned there were many other ways for the Xiiginns to bring a species under their dominion. The Humans were another such species. Some had the Mardoxian potential and the capacity to resist Xiiginn compulsion, but not all of them. Prax'pedax had come to accept that this was their last chance to engage in an effort to stop the Xiiginns for good. This is why they would fight to the last Boxan, even if there were those of the Boxan High Council who didn't fully understand. Mardoxian priests and priestesses, like Thesulia and Ma'jasalax, understood and worked to align events to that outcome. The alpha message sent back to command central would signal the dire need for the Boxans to send more ships to this star system. Though it would be too late for them, it might not be too late for Earth. The Humans would resist the Xiiginn invasion, though many of them would die in the process, and it was his job to take out as many of the Xiiginns as he could.

Prax'pedax shared a number of knowing looks with Thesulia. She had gambled on him coming to this realization and on his ability to convince all those Boxans under his command to follow him and make the ultimate sacrifice. Had he not seen the same conviction in his friend Kladomaor? Searching for remnant Drar technology, he might not have done as Thesulia advised. But knowing what he did now and glimpsing the insights only afforded to those of the Mardoxian sect gave him peace with his decisions.

He'd emptied his ship of shuttles, sending teams of Boxans

back to Earth to help them prepare. It would take the shuttles time to get back to Earth, but it was the best he could do and would give at least some Boxans under his command a fighting chance to survive and help the Humans prepare for the Xiiginns. He'd ordered Battle Commander Vuloyant to do the same thing on his ship. Shuttle capacity would hardly make a dent in the crew, but at least it was something.

"Battle Leader, the last long-range missile platforms have been deployed," Wynog reported.

"Excellent," Prax'pedax said. "Authorize the warfare system AI to upload instructions for the platforms to target computers. Maintain connections to keep targeting updated for as long as possible. Move our position back from the missile platforms."

"Confirm automatic refresh of targeting with warfare AI. Chain of command—primary, designate this ship, and backup, designate Battle Commander Vuloyant's ship's computer," Wynog said.

Prax'pedax's ship was designated the flagship of the two Dreadnaughts, and should his ship lose its capacity for combat, control would be passed to Vuloyant's ship. Should there be combat failure on both ships, targeting control would revert back to local targeting systems. Local targeting systems were much less effective than the powerful warfare AIs aboard a Dreadnaught ship's systems, but the redundancies were in place to maximize their effectiveness in combat.

"Signal close quarters combat active," Prax'pedax said.

He had leveraged his strike-fighters to protect the missile platforms while he waited to fire his long-range missiles. The Xiiginns had, in turn, sent their own slip-fighters to take out the missile platforms. Xiiginn warships had been steadily moving in closer ever since.

Prax'pedax had also leveraged combat drones to blind his enemy with jammers and decoys, and these had prevented the Xiiginns from being able to lock onto his ship. It was never easy to order soldiers under his command to fight until they could no longer fight. There would be no backup for any of them.

Prax'pedax monitored the long-range missile platforms as they depleted their payload into the oncoming Xiiginn warships. The molten fury from heavier warheads tore into the advancing fleet. Throughout the war with the Xiiginns, the Boxans had employed superior tactics, taking multitudes more of the enemy for each combat vessel, but the Xiiginns, with the support of various Confederation species, had simply overwhelmed Boxan battle groups time and time again through sheer numbers.

Prax'pedax activated a fleet-wide comms channel. "Boxans, the remaining Xiiginn fleet will be closing in on our ships. We will draw them in-system and take out as many as we can. We will unleash our battle song into the great expanse, and the Xiiginns will know the measure of our commitment to protect this star system. The Humans will know of our sacrifice, how we few held the line against the Xiiginn fleet and fought to the last Boxan. Our mission does not end here and will be carried on by those who come after us. We will keep fighting until there are none left to fight or the Xiiginns leave this star system."

Prax'pedax closed the comms channel. He had the utmost faith in his soldiers. They would fight and would not be cowed by the Xiiginns. He returned to his command couch. The pieces were in place, and now the battle would be fought in earnest.

A shock-lance of Xiiginn warships pushed forward into the welcoming fire of graser cannons and short-range missiles. The Dreadnaughts were ships of war, and they would deliver fire and death before this cycle was done.

CHAPTER THIRTY-SIX

Kaylan continued launch prep, polishing off the last checks. A comms channel opened from Engineering.

"Commander," Efren said, "energy readings from the reactor are orders of magnitude above what we had previously. It's as if the reactor is being fueled with an unknown material. I cannot guarantee that it's safe or what the capacity is there."

"Acknowledged, Efren. We'll be as careful as we can, but we need to go," Kaylan said.

She engaged the engines, and the Athena started away from the dock, moving at speeds much greater than when they'd come in. The crumbling Drar station was deteriorating all around them.

"The sensors are still showing a barrier ahead," Hicks said.

Kaylan frowned as she checked the sensor data. "Zack, I need you to disable the shroud here," she said.

"The sooner, the better," Hicks added.

There was silence, and Kaylan glanced around to see that Zack was frantically moving through the holo-interface.

"Hmm, that's . . . Wow!" Zack said.

"Zack," Kaylan called.

They were almost to the barrier.

"Command sent. Of course, I didn't realize there *was* a command to send until just now," Zack said.

A hole in the shroud barrier formed directly in front of them, and Kaylan watched as the barrier receded, exposing the inside to the vacuum of space. There were no telltale signs of an atmosphere escaping out of the hole. The countdown timer that had been on Kaylan's HUD adjusted itself, and they had less time to get away than before.

"Open a comms channel to Kladomaor," Kaylan said.

"Kladomaor?" Zack replied. "How do you even know he's . . . never mind."

Kaylan watched the navigation display showing them leaving the Drar space station behind and adjusted the scanners to the Boxan ship's frequency they'd had earlier.

"I'm not getting a reply," Zack said.

"I think I know why," Kaylan said. "Two ships are showing on the scanners."

Hicks glanced over at the screen and narrowed his gaze. "Looks like we've got company. Kladomaor might not be able to reply. We don't know what kind of damage they've sustained, but if he's trying to outrun the Xiiginns, he's not going to make it."

Kaylan took control of the comms interface and tried to reach out to Kladomaor. She plotted an intercept course, and it took only a few seconds to acknowledge that the Athena could move much faster than it could before.

A comms channel opened from the Boxan ship.

"Athena, this is Kladomaor. We're not going to make it. Cherubian drive is down. There . . . no escape . . . as long as we can," Kladomaor said.

The Boxan's deep voice kept going in and out.

"Kladomaor, we're heading to you. We have a way to get out of here. The Drars made changes to our ship, and we can get back to Earth, but we're not going to leave you behind," Kaylan said.

"It's too dangerous. The Xiiginns are almost upon us . . ." Kladomaor said.

"Listen to me," Kaylan shouted. "All you have to do is have the gravity tether working. Once we reach you, engage the tether and the Athena can take us both out of here."

"Cannot . . . tether . . . unreliable . . ."

The comms channel went dead.

Kaylan glanced helplessly at Hicks and then looked at the navigation computer. They were speeding toward Kladomaor's ship. She scanned the systems to see if there was anything in the new functions that resembled a gravity tether, cursing in frustration.

"Damn it. The Drars gave us all this new equipment, and we can't even use it to save the others," Kaylan said.

Hicks was searching, too.

"I can't find anything either," Zack said.

They had the location of Earth from Kladomaor's ship's computers. Those coordinates were meant for a Cherubian drive but were already in the Athena's system. The navigation computer allowed her to enter those coordinates and gave an almost instant feedback of acceptance.

"The communications choked at the end. Let's get there and see if the Boxans have one last trick up their sleeves," Hicks said.

Kaylan nodded and fixed her gaze on the plotted course.

"Zack—" Kaylan began to say.

"I already got sensor arrays for the gravitonics set up. If they get the tether working, I'll let you know," Zack said.

"Now, if only the Drar AI had given us some weapons systems. I keep looking but haven't found anything," Hicks said.

Kaylan hadn't expected the Drar AI to give them any weapons, but she couldn't be sure. There was nothing for them to do but wait, hope, and pray.

The Athena closed in on the Boxans, and Kaylan's mouth hung open at the sight of the battle-weary ship. Large sections of the Boxan ship had been torn apart. Kaylan didn't know how it was still holding together. She glanced back at Zack, and he shook his head. No gravity tether. She'd tried to reach Klado-maor again, but there had been no reply. The only thing she saw was the Xiiginn ship moving steadily closer and the countdown from the Drar space station getting closer to zero. They were going to have to leave or they would die.

Kaylan watched the timer drain away, waiting to engage the coordinates to Earth.

"Yes!" Zack shouted. "Tether engaged!"

Kaylan engaged the nav computer. Directly in front of them, the view seemed to fold away from itself, and she watched the energy output from the reactor spike.

The status on the HUD read 'wormhole established.'

The Athena lurched ahead, dragging the battle-torn Boxan ship in its wake, but they weren't out of danger yet. She focused her attention on the countdown timer as it reached zero, keeping the sensors active and watching for any signs of the Drar space station explosion following them.

Zack walked to the back of her chair. "This doesn't feel like any wormhole we've gone through before."

He was right. Going through wormholes using the Cherubian drive normally left them disoriented. They were still in transit, but there was no disorientation.

"What are you scanning for?" Zack asked.

"Jonah stayed behind to engage the Drar self-destruct. The AI couldn't do it on its own," Kaylan said.

Zack's eyes drew downward, and Kaylan saw emotion well up in his gaze.

"I think we're clear," Kaylan said. "And there's no sign of the Xiiginn ship following us."

"They likely got caught in the explosion. There's no way they could have known it was coming," Hicks said.

An alarm came to prominence on Kaylan's holoscreen, warning that transit time was about to deplete. They were almost home. Kaylan knew from her time aboard Kladomaor's ship that, as a safety precaution, wormholes were only opened outside a star system. The door to the bridge opened and the rest of the crew entered, with the exception of Efren and Nikolai, who remained in Engineering.

"We're about to come out of transit," Kaylan said.

They were excited. The thought of finally getting back to Earth, even if they were only at the fringes of their solar system, was enough to make them all happy. Zack squeezed her shoulder, and she took his hand while smiling up at him.

They emerged from the wormhole directly into a nightmare the likes of which they could never have dreamed possible.

"Oh my god!" Kaylan gasped.

The crew of the Athena was stunned as they watched bright explosions continually light up in the distance. They'd emerged into the middle of the battle with the Xiiginn fleet.

Across the galaxy, in a remnant planetoid spaceship, the Drar artificial intelligence leveraged its newfound entity with the designation Jonah Redford. The entity monitored for the presence of the ship called the Athena until it disappeared, but there was one foreign spaceship outside the shroud when the entity delivered on its promise. The power core from the planetoid spaceship went into critical overload and exploded, unleashing the exponential force of the old dwarf star that had powered it for millions of years.

CHAPTER THIRTY-SEVEN

Michael Hunsicker rubbed his eyes and took his last swig of coffee. It hadn't taken him long to become accustomed to having coffee regularly again. On the lunar base, it was hard for him to acclimate to what constituted daytime and nighttime. Usually he could adapt just fine, but his difficulty was because of all the hours he'd spent working with Chazen and the other Boxans who had taken up residence at the base. Some of the Boxans had set up some temporary housing that connected to the base's complex on the lunar surface. This helped out because, while they could accommodate the Boxans, it was quite evident that the original designers of the lunar base never imagined that a ten-foot-tall alien race would be in residence there.

He'd become an unofficial liaison between the Boxans and the Humans on the base. Edward Johnson had contacted him many times to ask his opinion about the Boxan position on different issues, but those calls had slowed down considerably with the onset of asteroids being hurled at their planet. Even the asteroids seemed to have slowed down, with one rather large exception. The orbital protection grid managed to nullify the threat of the smaller asteroids, but it was the large one only a few days from destroying the Earth that occupied all their attention.

Michael glanced over at Chazen. "Any thoughts on the Xiiginns using these tactics on us?"

Chazen looked at a Boxan named Alark, who was an actual Boxan soldier. Michael had never seen Alark out of his powered armor.

"The Xiiginns use fear to defeat their enemies. I don't think they intend the asteroid to destroy your planet, hence the reason the trajectory is a bit off for a direct hit. They're engaged in a battle with Prax'pedax, and they either expected to overwhelm our forces quickly, arriving in time to stop the asteroid, or they're willing to accept a substantial loss of population. They only need some of you alive to enslave," Alark said.

Michael felt his mouth go dry. The soldier's unapologetic tone had surprised more than one person here, but Michael had come to expect it. Alark had already confirmed that they didn't have the armament available to destroy the moon-sized asteroid. There had to be another way.

A comms channel opened on the ECF-encrypted communications channel. One of the first things the ECF had done was send out a new set of encryption protocols so they could communicate on a secure channel. The protocols were updated to use the Boxan comms devices, so there was virtually no chance of someone being able to decrypt their communications.

"Lunar Base, this is the Endurance," Commander Matthews said.

Alissa put a headset on and engaged the comms channel. "Go ahead, Endurance. This is Lunar Base actual," she said.

"We've finished preliminary mapping of the asteroid surface and have found some interesting things. It looks like the Xiiginns put engines on the thing, and that's what's pushing the asteroid along. My team has come up with a firing solution, but I didn't want to take any action without running it by some of those smart people we have on our side. Transmitting the images we have of the engines," Commander Matthews said.

"Acknowledged. Endurance, give us few minutes to see what you've got," Alissa said.

"Engines pushing the asteroid along," Michael said. "He's right to wait."

"Agreed," Alissa said and opened the comms channel back up. "Endurance, waiting is a good idea. I'm going to patch in General Sheridan and his staff. Just give us a few minutes to bring them up to speed."

"Acknowledged," Commander Matthews said.

Michael looked over at Alark. "Do you know anything about the type of engines the Xiiginns could be using to push the asteroid along?" he asked.

Alissa sat next to him but was talking to ECF command central.

They received the transmitted images of what looked like an engine farm residing on the surface of the asteroid. Alark peered at the image and frowned.

"They can be remote controlled, but the command-and-control function will only be available on a Xiiginn warship and cannot be duplicated," Alark said.

Alissa had been listening to their conversation while she waited on General Sheridan.

After a few moments, the general came on the line.

"Did I hear that correctly? The Endurance has photographed engines on the surface of the asteroid?" General Sheridan said.

"That's correct, sir. We've run some numbers, and we do have a firing solution to take out the engines," Commander Matthews said.

"Don't do that," another voice said. "I'm sorry, General, this is Gary Hunter again. Don't let them take out the engines."

"Why the hell not?" the general asked.

"This is good news," Gary said. There was the sound of other people talking and Gary's response to them. "That's right, they've got an image of a bunch of engines on the asteroid surface. I know. I'll tell them if you'll quit talking to me." Gary cleared his throat. "I'm sorry about that, but we think that if you can give us some images of the asteroid, along with its current trajectory, we can tell you which engines to take out."

"What would disabling only some of the engines accomplish?" the general asked.

"Think of it this way. The Boxans might be able to confirm this, but an engine farm, or array of engines, pushing something as big as that asteroid must be configured to a specific amount of thrust. If we take out only some of the engines on a particular side, we might be able to get the asteroid to miss Earth entirely, but if we do it wrong, it will just start spinning out of control," Gary said.

"Get to work, Hunter. I want those numbers triple-checked. Whatever you need, you've got it. Now get off the comms channel and get to work," the general said.

Michael looked at Chazen, who had brought up his own holo-interface and begun running his own simulations.

"Your scientist is correct," Chazen said.

Commander Kyle Matthews stood on the bridge of the Endurance. He'd been tasked with the retrofit of the Endurance's design to make the ship into a military ship. His military rank was colonel, but in space, the leader of a spaceship or mission was referred to as the commander. He fully expected that this would change once the ECF got off the ground.

Outside the windows of the ship, a behemoth of an asteroid dominated the view. In its path was their home. The crew of the Endurance had run their own numbers and, together with the ECF, they had a firing solution.

"Target engines identified," Alan said.

"Fire," Kyle ordered.

Missiles launched from their tubes on the external missile platform. The payloads were enough to disable the engines on the asteroid, and there was very little room for error. The theory was that if they took out enough engines, the thrust coming from the remaining engines would change the asteroid's trajectory, but causing the asteroid to spin uncontrollably was a real concern.

He watched the holoscreen, waiting for the detonation confirmation that the missiles had reached their intended targets. They only had one shot at this, and there were no more missiles. Kyle glanced at Alan, his pilot, and knew that the rest of the crew was waiting for confirmation.

"Confirmed detonation. All birds have reached their destination," Lewis reported from the comms station.

Kyle blew out a breath.

"Endurance, we received confirmed detonation signal. Do you have a visual?" Alissa Archer's voice came over the comms channel from the lunar base.

Kyle climbed out of the command chair and went over to the conference table. The image of the engine farm was still buffering. Alan and Lewis joined him. Multiple targets were destroyed, but as the image finished loading, they realized that they had taken out too many engines.

"Oh no," Alan said and kept repeating it as he plugged in the updated numbers. "That's too many. That's too many."

A smaller holoscreen appeared with the three-dimensional model of the asteroid that NASA and the other space agencies had used in planning. The updated numbers showed that they'd taken out many more engines than they'd planned. The probability model updated, showing that the asteroid would still hit the Earth.

"How could this have happened? The payload for those missiles shouldn't have taken out anywhere near that many engines," Lewis said.

Kyle felt his stomach sink to his feet. Instead of saving the Earth, they might have just signed its death warrant. He brought his hand up and rubbed his chin in thought. Then his eyes narrowed. "They would if they were set up to be sabotaged."

Alan's eyes widened. "You mean to tell me that they anticipated our attack and had some kind of redundancy in place to keep the asteroid on course?"

Kyle blew out a breath and gave him nod. His mouth went

dry as he opened up a comms channel. "Lunar Base, are you seeing this?" he asked.

There was a long moment of silence as they waited for the reply.

"Confirmed, Endurance. Stand by," Alissa said.

Kyle could tell her throat was thick with emotion. He felt the same thing. He clenched his hands into fists and muted the comms channel to the lunar base.

"Options," Kyle said. "Anything. Anything you've got. I don't care how crazy it is. We've got nothing to lose at this point. I'd smash this ship against it if I thought it would do any good."

Kyle racked his brain, trying to come up with something. He watched as Alan and Lewis did the same.

"Hell, we've got engines on this ship, and I'd use them if it would help," Kyle said, pacing around the conference table.

Lewis frowned in thought. "That might not be a bad idea," he said.

Kyle watched as Lewis brought up a smaller holoscreen and began running some calculations. Lewis was among the smartest men Kyle knew. He worked well under pressure and wouldn't have been assigned to the Endurance if he hadn't been able to run calculations.

"We should probably check my numbers. It's possible, but we have to do it now, and . . ." Lewis stopped speaking and gave them a long look.

"We'll destroy the ship in the process," Kyle said.

Lewis nodded.

"What about tactical nukes? Send them up from Earth—" Alan said.

Lewis shook his head. "No, they'll never get here in time, and we're not sure if that will even work."

"Let's keep that as a backup plan if we fail," Kyle said and opened a comms channel for a ship-wide broadcast. "The missiles have failed. We took out too many of the engines. We have another solution, but it will require us to sacrifice the Endurance. We're going to try and nudge the asteroid with the ship. It's a long shot. Some would consider it a one-in-a-million chance, but it's all we can do with the time given to us. I want you all to get into your EVA suits. I'm going to send an update to ECF, and then we're going to push this big bitch out of the way so our homes and families get to live. Commander out," Kyle said.

He recorded a message and waited to send it to the lunar base. By the time he was done, Lewis and Alan were in their EVA suits and were working on a slow approach vector to get the Endurance into position. They had to disable the safeguards in the main computer before they'd be allowed to plot the course. Kyle put on his own EVA suit. The fact that he was able to do so while on the bridge was one of the design improvements they'd made over the Athena.

Alan was about to take his seat when Lewis called out to him.

"We can't do this from the bridge," Lewis said.

Kyle nodded. "Right, because it's in the front of the ship."

"Well, we need to get the ship into position first, and that can only be done from here," Alan said and sat in the pilot's seat.

Kyle turned toward Lewis. "Why don't you get set up in the med bay, and we'll join you after we get the ship in position."

Lewis let out a snort. "Like hell I'll leave you two up here. We do this together."

Kyle smiled and gave Lewis a nod.

"Plus, I'm not sure Alan can pull this off without my help. What if he needs some last-minute calculations? I think he barely passed flight school. How'd he even get assigned to this cush mission anyway?" Lewis said.

Alan chuckled while doing some last-minute checks, while Kyle took a few seconds to just be in the moment and acknowledge the fear he was feeling and the staunch determination and hope that their sacrifice would mean something. He thought of his daughters Taliya and Melayna, both in high school. He saw their beautiful, smiling faces, along with his wife. He'd been so busy with the Endurance that he'd hardly seen them during the past six months. He closed his eyes and imagined them all sitting around the fire pit he'd built in the backyard of his home, with a clear sky above them and a warm fire to keep the chill of the night away. He recorded a video log for his family, his throat becoming thick with emotion, but he managed to say his good-byes. He urged the rest of the crew to do the same.

"We're all set, Commander. Flight is go," Alan said.

Kyle listened as the rest of the crew checked in.

"All messages have been sent, Commander," Lewis said in a somber tone. "Sorry . . ."

"There is nothing to be sorry about," Kyle said. "We have a job to do. We're here, and it's ours."

There was a moment of silence. "Go," Kyle said.

The Endurance had been holding its position above the ruined engine farm. The Xiiginns had picked a relatively flat surface on which to stage the engines. Alan brought the

Endurance in at an angle and put the nose of the ship on the rocky crevice. They'd used probes to take samples from the surface and knew that while the large asteroid was half the size of the moon, it was nowhere near as dense. The gravitational pull from the asteroid was marginal. The approach took a lot of time, with the asteroid surface slowly becoming the only thing they could see outside the windows of the bridge.

"Firing maneuvering thrusters," Alan said.

Throughout all their training for every conceivable scenario that NASA and the other space agencies could come up with, this had not been among them. To calm the others down, Kyle had told them to treat this as a docking procedure. They were merely lining up the front of the ship to dock with another ship. Putting their insurmountable task in those terms allowed the rest of the crew to wrap their minds around what they were doing. Suddenly, they were able to focus, and the impossible became possible.

"Threading the needle," Alan murmured to himself. "I'm a leaf on the wind."

"I can't believe you're still quoting that old show," Lewis said.

"You'll understand one day," Alan answered.

Kyle remained quiet and continued to monitor their approach. Alan's hands were steady as the surface of the asteroid drew closer, and the Endurance came to a crunching halt. A combination of thrusters was holding the Endurance in place.

"Stage one, complete," Kyle said.

"Stage two, mark," Alan said.

Though they couldn't hear it, Kyle watched the slow but steady rise in the rear main engine's thrust.

"Time for you to go, Lewis," Kyle said.

Lewis climbed out of the chair and left the bridge.

After a few moments, Kyle said, "Alan, you too. I've got this."

"Commander?" Alan said.

"I don't need a pilot for this. I just need to monitor and adjust something if necessary. Go. That's an order," Kyle said.

Alan gave him a hard look. "I'll help Lewis with getting the med bay set up as a backup bridge. Once we're ready, you don't need to stay up here."

Kyle nodded, and Alan left the bridge. After a few moments watching the steady increase in main engine output, he climbed out of the chair and moved toward the conference table. He could monitor the feeds from there. Future designs of spacecraft should include a secondary bridge, and perhaps not putting the primary bridge at the very front of the spacecraft might be a design improvement too. Kyle glanced up at the drone data feed on the holodisplay. They'd launched several smaller drones that were tasked with tracking the asteroid and its trajectory toward Earth, and he'd harbored a foolish hope that it would change, but the logical part of his brain told him it was too soon. Kyle updated the main engine thrust so it increased faster. There was a loud groan caused by the straining support structure of the spacecraft. The steady increase of force was going to crush the front of the ship.

"Commander, get off the bridge, now! Hull integrity compromised," Alan's voice came over comms.

Kyle took a last long look at the bridge of the Endurance. There had been so many hopes and dreams that had gone into the making of this ship, and he felt a profound sense of regret that its life would be cut off before it really had a chance to live.

"You have to get out of there now, or you'll be crushed like an old soda can—"

"Keep your pants on. I'm coming," Kyle said.

He opened the door to the bridge, then closed it behind him and sealed the bridge. As he made his way through the ship, he saw that the crew had already locked the ship down, and he found most of them assembled in the mess hall. They'd elected not to use the shuttle to escape in order to also leverage its small thrust capabilities against the asteroid. They would use everything at their disposal. The crew of the Endurance waited in silence. Lewis had set up several holoscreens so they could monitor and control what systems they could through the redundant switchover in the event of emergencies.

Kyle watched as engine thrust was nearing seventy-five percent of capacity. They were pushing a moving object in space, and while it increased the speed that the asteroid was moving, it was having very little effect on the trajectory. Lewis kept updating the data model he'd put together using the current data feeds and then set it to auto-refresh, watching with the rest of them. The original design of the spacecraft had taken into account the unlikely event of the ship colliding with another object in space. The engineers hadn't had what they were trying to do here in mind, but the principles of impactful forces were still the same. In essence, in the event of catastrophic failure, each part of the Endurance was designed to fail in a certain way. Each compartment could withstand the sudden loss of atmospheric pressure and the stresses of prolonged space travel. So when the forward compartment failed due to the massive pressures exerted while trying to move a large asteroid, the area where the bridge was would flatten like an accordion. The central and rear sections of the ship were much sturdier than the forward, rounded section of the front of the ship, having been designed to withstand the huge thrust capability coming from the rear main engines. It was this and this alone that allowed the crew of the Endurance to survive for longer than even they had expected.

Kyle kept his eyes on Lewis's holoscreen. More than an hour had passed since they'd started this crazy plan, and the trajectory of the asteroid had slightly altered. Unfortunately, it wasn't enough. All probability calculations still had an asteroid half the size of the moon clipping the south pole of the Earth. There was nothing for them to do but wait for the inevitable impact that would destroy them and the Earth, or for the hull integrity to fail, in which case they would all die. They chewed up the time by telling stories, tension letting up for a few seconds until the data feeds refreshed the reports. At least they were together and knew what was going to happen. Kyle wondered what the people of Earth knew. They could see the asteroid in the night sky, but the ECF had understandably kept them in the dark. Kyle didn't know if people had succumbed to despair, beginning the fundamental breakdown of society as they knew it, but he chose to believe that people were together, that his wife and daughters were together with the rest of the family—scared, to be sure, but none of them would die alone.

"Commander, I'm getting a comms signal," Lewis said.

Kyle started to make his way through the crowded mess hall and stopped. "Do you know who it is? Can you put it on one of these screens?"

"Audio only," Lewis said.

Static could be heard from speakers in the mess hall.

"Crew of the Endurance, this is Scraanyx, Strike

Commander serving under Battle Leader Prax'pedax. We've analyzed your efforts, and we're lining up for our final approach to assist. Stand by."

Kyle's eyes widened in shock. He looked at Lewis questioningly, but Lewis's eyes were glued to the screen.

"Oh my god! They're the Boxan shuttles from the Dreadnaughts . . ." Lewis said, his eyes growing misty. "There are sixty of them. They're positioning themselves all along the equatorial plane."

"Is it enough?" Kyle asked, hardly daring to breathe.

Lewis licked his lips, looking from the holoscreen in front of him and then back up at the rest of the crew. "I don't know. I'm not sure what their shuttle capabilities are, but I've got to believe it will help."

Kyle looked at the faces of the Endurance crew with a mixture of awe and a growing feeling of hope. They couldn't tell anyone, but their chances of nudging this behemoth had just substantially increased.

CHAPTER THIRTY-EIGHT

Z ack watched his third space battle unfold from the bridge of the Athena. Of all the homecoming scenarios he could have imagined, watching a fleet of Xiiginn warships throw themselves at two of the biggest ships he'd ever seen wasn't one of them. The whole thing looked like a fake light show, but the actuality of Boxan blood being scattered into space stunned them all into silence.

Zack looked at Kaylan and the others. All of them were completely at a loss as to what to do. What could they do? They were relatively close to the solar system, but Zack knew they were beyond Pluto's orbit, which, incidentally, was still near the sun. He'd patched the Athena's computers into the Boxan systems, and one of the things still working on Kladomaor's ship was its onboard sensor suite. The electronic warfare AI began identifying targets on the battlefield. Zack didn't need to be a soldier to recognize that the Xiiginns had brought an overwhelming force and were pushing toward the Boxan ships of the designation Dreadnaught.

Zack brought his hands up to his head and pushed his hair back. "We've got to do something," he said.

Kaylan opened a comms channel to the Boxan ship. "Klado-maor, are you seeing this?"

"The sensors are showing us that two of our Dreadnaughts have engaged the Xiiginn fleet," Kladomaor said.

Zack scanned the output on the holoscreen. "What are all those things scattered behind the fleet?"

"Those are the ships that have been destroyed," Kladomaor said.

Zack was about to ask another question, but Hicks raised his finger to his lips. Kaylan put the comms channel on mute so Kladomaor couldn't hear them.

"The Xiiginns are throwing themselves at those Boxan ships, and it looks like they will overwhelm them any minute now," Hicks said.

"We can't stay here," Kladomaor said.

Kaylan looked around at all of them. Zack wanted to do something to give her hope. The Drars had changed their ship, but they still didn't understand everything that had been done. They'd just traveled who knows how many light years to get back home, and now it looked as if they were about to witness the full-on invasion of the solar system.

"It looks like the Boxans sent some protection for Earth, but not even they anticipated what the Xiiginns would bring," Hicks said.

"We can't even reach Earth from way out here. The smallest message would take hours to get there," Kaylan said.

Zack frowned in thought. He wanted to take Kaylan into his arms and tell her everything was going to be okay, that somehow they'd find a way through all this, but he knew that wasn't the case. If only there were some way they could protect themselves.

"Protection!" Zack shouted. "We need protection," he said.

He raced back to the comms station. Kaylan and the others on the bridge bunched together behind him.

"Damn screens are too small," Zack said, springing out of the chair. "Just give me a second," he said while weaving his way to the conference table.

The large holodisplay came on, and Zack's fingers flew through the interface.

Kladomaor asked if they were still there, and Kaylan told him they needed a minute.

"What are you doing?" Kaylan asked.

"I might have a way to protect the Earth from the Xiiginns," Zack said. He continued to bring up multiple windows, each with their own set of tasks running. "It has to be there somewhere . . ."

"Is there something we can do to help?" Hicks asked.

Zack glanced at him for a moment. "Yes, I need you to monitor exactly where the fighting is happening. I'll need the precise location."

"But what is—" Hicks started to say.

"I'm sorry. We can talk, or we can do," Zack said.

He hated cutting Hicks off, but he needed to focus. Hicks brought up a secondary holodisplay away from where Zack was working, and Kaylan stood next to him, watching him work.

"You're in the Boxan system. What are you looking for in there?" Kaylan asked.

"The command and control for the shroud network," Zack said.

"But Kladomaor wouldn't have that on his ship," Kaylan said.

"You're right, but the listening post has it. The data upload I took from it was partial. It's like knowing half a language, but on the way here, when you had me open the shroud around the Drar space station, I got to thinking that maybe we can do something similar with our Star Shroud. Kladomaor said it's based on the Drar technology they'd found," Zack said.

"That's right, but I don't think the shroud can block the Xiiginn fleet. The Drars had defensive measures in place," Kaylan said.

Zack smiled at her. "Just wait while . . . there it goes. Signal broadcast in three . . . two . . . one."

They waited a few moments, and a comms channel opened from Engineering.

"Commander, we're seeing a huge spike in power output. What are you guys doing?" Efren asked.

"It's going to the comms system," Zack said.

"Just keep monitoring it, Efren," Kaylan said, and she looked back at Zack.

"I'm realigning the shroud devices. When we were leaving the Drar space station, I saw the protocols used there. It's in our system. They meant for us to have it. It was the only way we were getting out of there, and it just might help us here," Zack said.

Kaylan's eyes lit up in understanding. "You're realigning the shroud devices to form a shield around the entire solar system. How do you know the devices can get here in time? And where are you telling the devices to go?"

"To your first question, I'm not sure. I'm thinking it's pretty fast. As to your second question, just beyond the fighting," Zack said.

"But we'll be trapped on the other side with the Xiiginn fleet," Hicks called out.

Zack frowned.

"We have to move the ship. Tell Kladomaor to re-engage the tether," Kaylan said.

"No, wait. We can't move. We have to stay right where we are. The broadcast . . . I don't . . . We can't move. I don't know what will happen if we try to beat the shroud devices," Zack said.

"How long do we have?" Kaylan asked.

"Once we're in the shroud network, it will help cascade the message across to other devices but—" Zack said.

Kaylan ran to the pilot's seat. "We have to try," she said.

Warning alarms blared. There were multiple proximity alarms from approaching objects from the Oort Cloud. The sensors showed an immense wave of contacts beyond the scope of what the sensors were capable of reporting, and they were converging right toward them. A bright light flared outside the Athena's windows, followed by another one equally as bright. Their sensors were overwhelmed, and the screens blanked out from data overload.

CHAPTER THIRTY-NINE

M ar Arden monitored the battle from the bridge of the warship under Hoan Berend's command. They'd been placed on the outskirts of the battle and were witnessing the slaughter of multiple Xiiginn ships. But for each ship destroyed, they were diminishing the Boxans' capacity to fight. Garm Antis wouldn't let the Boxans stand in the way of the Human star system, but one thing Mar Arden had seen time and time again from the Boxans was that when they committed to a course of action, they would fight to the bitter end.

Mar Arden went over to Hoan Berend, and Kandra Rene followed him.

"What's the status of the anomalous wormhole wake that was detected?" Mar Arden asked.

Hoan Berend looked over at him. "It has a signature unlike anything we've ever seen. I've reported it up the command chain. They're not sure what it is. Since it's not an immediate threat, it won't be investigated until after we crush the Boxans."

Mar Arden clenched his teeth. If there was one thing he'd learned from his recent encounters with Kladomaor, it was that there were no chance occurrences that didn't warrant their full attention. He could push the issue with Hoan Berend, but the commander had already taken the appropriate action.

Kandra Rene moved toward the comms officer station and looked over Berend's shoulder, then glanced back at Mar Arden. "There's a powerful comms signal being sent out," Kandra Rene said.

Mar Arden walked over and took a look. "It could be just another decoy attempting to divide our forces," he said.

Hoan Berend nodded. "You could be right."

"At last we agree on something. The fighting is just about finished. Why don't we move farther into the system?" Mar Arden said.

"Our orders are to stay right here," Hoan Berend said.

Mar Arden looked away and sneered, then gripped his pistol and launched himself at the commander. He was on him in seconds, slamming the point of his pistol into the commander's head. Several of the soldiers drew their weapons and started heading toward their fallen commander, but Kandra Rene blocked their path with her own weapons.

"I'm taking command of this ship, you fool," Mar Arden said. He slammed the pistol down on Hoan Berend's head and then flung the unconscious commander from his chair. "This ship is now under my command."

One of the tactical officers stood up. "You can't—"

His statement was cut short when Mar Arden shot him. He hadn't eliminated Hoan Berend because he still had his uses, but any junior officer was fair game.

"Is there anyone else who'd challenge my authority?" Mar Arden said and leveled his gaze at the soldiers.

They put their weapons away and waited.

"Good," Mar Arden said. "Take Hoan Berend to his quarters and stand guard. Alert me when he wakes up."

Two of the soldiers came forward and carried the unconscious Xiiginn from the bridge.

"Navigation, take us into the system, best speed," Mar Arden said.

He gave Kandra Rene a nod and sat in the commander's chair.

"Commander, tactical is detecting multiple contacts," the Xiiginn tactical officer said.

"Put it on screen," Mar Arden said.

The main holodisplay showed a chaotic view of what looked like a swarm of tiny ships that were already at their position. Mar Arden's tail twitched. He couldn't make sense of what he was seeing.

"Divert all power to the engines," Mar Arden said.

The warship lurched forward, and he watched the swarm gather, forming some kind of barrier in front of the main fleet. None of the other ships were launching ahead like they were. They would wait for Garm Antis to give the order.

As the first of the Xiiginn ships made contact with the swarm, their onboard responder abruptly cut off, signaling the total destruction of their ship.

Mar Arden's eyes rounded in fear as he glanced at the readout showing the swarm gathering in front of their ship. Master alarms blared as if they'd been taking damage in battle.

Tactical engaged the point defense systems, and for a brief

moment they fired their weapons back at whatever was trying to form around them. Main power cut out, plunging the bridge into total darkness, and the emergency power went on.

"Go to individual life support," Mar Arden shouted.

He engaged his helmet, which instantly formed around his head, and saw Kandra Rene and the other bridge officers do the same. Then a massive hull breach tore into the bridge.

CHAPTER FORTY

The navigation computer wouldn't accept any course from Kaylan that took them toward Earth. She tried manual override of the controls, and Hicks asked her to wait. It took more than a few minutes for the Athena's AI to sort through all the sensor data. They'd watched the holodisplay as the Star Shroud devices realigned closer in the system.

Kaylan couldn't decide if it had been luck or fate that had led the Boxans to start using the devices they called the Star Shroud. The devices were based on Drar technology that the Boxans hadn't changed much since they'd found the original prototypes hundreds of years ago. It was for that reason alone that the shroud devices accepted the Drar protocols, enabling additional functionality not even Kladomaor or Gaarokk knew existed. They watched as most of the remaining Xiiginn fleet slammed into the newly formed shroud barrier. The ships in the Xiiginn fleet nearest the barrier had no warning and were instantly destroyed, but the ships in the very rear of the fleet formation were able to take evasive maneuvers.

Kaylan tried to send a communication toward Earth, but couldn't lock in the signal. She should have known it was too much to hope for.

She kept a close eye on Zack. She didn't think he'd known what he was doing at the time, but his actions had caused the deaths of thousands of Xiiginns. His expression went from horror to grim satisfaction and then back to surprise.

"Athena," Kladomaor's voice came over the speakers on the bridge.

"Go ahead," Kaylan said.

"We detected multiple Boxan signals in the system before we were cut off. There is a strong probability that there are Boxans on Earth," Kladomaor said.

"That's good to hear, but we can't get through the barrier. Zack tried to use the same protocols we used to escape the Drar space station, but it's not working," Kaylan said.

"Hmm," Kladomaor said. "It could be that it only works from inside the shroud."

Kaylan glanced at Zack and Hicks.

"It's possible. I really don't know. I just wanted to keep the Xiiginns from reaching Earth. I didn't even think about being locked outside of it," Zack said.

"We can't stay here," Kladomaor said.

Kaylan looked at the Athena's crew. A short while ago they'd been full of hope that they'd finally be able to go back home, and now they were trapped outside the Star Shroud.

"He's right," Hicks said. "The remaining Xiiginn ships are

going to notice us at any moment, and we're in no condition to fight."

There was a general voice of agreement.

"I don't even know where we should go," Kaylan said. "Where can we go? We can't get back home, and we have no way of communicating with Earth."

Kaylan's shoulders slumped. She just wanted it all to stop. Everything they'd been through had led to this moment, and she couldn't fault Zack for doing what had to be done. There hadn't been time for them to get safely in the system and then engage the Star Shroud.

"We've gotten this far," Hicks said. "We can go a little farther."

Kaylan drew in a deep breath. She was the commander, but there was no way she could go on without the crew. An unbreakable bond had been forged among all of them. She noted Jonah Redford's absence, and she found that she missed the arrogant astrophysicist who'd sacrificed himself so they could escape the Drar space station. He'd known he was going to die anyway. The damage done to his brain by the Xiiginn compulsion had been irreversible, but he was still one of them. Part of the Athena's crew.

"We have a suggestion," Kladomaor said. "Ma'jasalax and I, that is."

"What is it?" Kaylan asked.

"We would suggest that we go to our colony. We find ourselves in need of your help since there is no way for us to get there without your ship," Kladomaor said.

Kaylan felt her lips lift in a small smile. "Quite a turn of events. Of course we'll help you. We can't stay here, and we need to better understand what the Drars did to our ship."

"We appreciate your help. The Drars have bestowed a great gift. They've deemed you worthy," Kladomaor said.

"I'm not sure it was actually the Drars. I think their AI was terribly lonely after waiting for so long, and it had gained some sentience—enough to know that it wanted to end its long existence but couldn't without help. It showed us a lot," Kaylan said and shared a look with Brenda Goodwin.

"They deemed you worthy; otherwise, you would have never been given access to the space station in the first place," Kladomaor said with an air of finality. "As to our current situation, there are no direct wormholes to our colony world. Its location is our most precious secret. We have to go to an interim point and then be granted access. I think the Boxan High Council would be eager to meet all of you, and together we can decide a way forward."

Kaylan looked out the window, and where the sun should have been was an area of distorted space. Zack came over to her.

"I'm sorry I couldn't get us home," Zack said.

"Don't apologize. You did what had to be done. Now at least the people of Earth will have a reprieve from the threat of invasion," Kaylan said.

"How are they even going to know what happened? What we did . . . What I did?" Zack said.

"You heard Kladomaor," Hicks said. "There are other Boxans inside the system. They'll work with the people back home to sort it out. A lot has happened in a short amount of time, and we need some time to process it all."

Kaylan nodded. "Hicks is right. First things first. Let's get to safety and then take it from there."

Kladomaor sent them the coordinates, which would be the first of several destinations before they could chance going to the Boxan colony world. She couldn't fault his caution—somehow the Xiiginns had tracked them to the Drar space station. She entered the coordinates into the navigation computer, and the Drar version of the Cherubian drive came online. A wormhole opened in front of the two ships, and they disappeared before the remnants of the Xiiginn fleet could regroup and investigate their presence.

CHAPTER FORTY-ONE

M ar Arden led a team of surviving Xiiginn soldiers moving through the hulking wreck that had been their warship. They still didn't know what had happened, but the surviving Xiiginns did know that the only reason any of them were still alive was because of Mar Arden's quick thinking and actions. Before they'd lost main power throughout the ship, Mar Arden had seen the fleet slam against some type of massive barrier. Where had the Boxans gotten such a weapon? Why hadn't they used it before? They'd fought and drawn the fleet toward them, sacrificing two of their Dreadnaught-class starships in the battle. Garm Antis had trapped a third Dreadnaught. The commander of that ship had fought to the bitter end, taking as many Xiiginns as they could. It wasn't enough. Nothing the Boxans could do was enough to stop the Xiiginn empire. Until now, that is, but the tactics still didn't make any sense. He kept working through the events while the teams of soldiers and bridge officers went through the ship, finding survivors and gathering supplies. Kandra Rene led a team to assess the damage in Engineering. It was one thing for the main power to go offline, but for the backup redundant systems to fail was quite another.

The more he thought about the Boxan tactics, the more he thought that this mysterious barrier had nothing to do with them. It was the only explanation that made any sense. Following this line of thought brought him back to the anomalous wormhole detection. The computer systems were down, so he couldn't get to any of the information they had on it, but he remembered the tactical officer commenting that it had a signature unlike anything they'd seen before. Preliminary analysis of Human technology had shown no indication that they possessed anything like the Cherubian drive, but Mar Arden's instincts connected the anomalous wormhole and the barrier. Two technological feats they hadn't come across before indicated that there was another species in this war—a new player—and their presence left the way open for all sorts of possibilities.

The short-range scanners reported that the barrier was still in place, but they were inside its confines. They couldn't reach any other ships in the fleet, so it was safe to assume that they were the only Xiiginns who'd made it through the barrier. Chances were that the Boxans on the Human home world called Earth didn't know they were here either, which gave them an advantage.

Mar Arden drew in a deep breath and blew it out. They could only leverage the advantage of surprise if they could make it to Earth undetected. In the not-too-distant past, Kladomaor had led a small team to the Nershal star system with the intention of igniting a rebellion against the Xiiginns. Those tactics had been a marked deviation from what the Boxans had used before, but given the situation they were in, he thought those same tactics would serve the Xiiginns' cause as well. They needed to salvage what they could from this wreck and hide it.

Kandra Rene opened a comms channel to him.

"Go ahead," Mar Arden said.

"We can't get to Engineering or any other part of the rear of the ship because those sections are gone," Kandra Rene said.

"Understood, continue sweeping the area for survivors. We're going to need everyone we can for what comes next," Mar Arden said.

"I would like to ask a question," Kandra Rene said.

Mar Arden had no doubt that she had many questions. "Go ahead," he said.

"What could the Boxans have done that could literally tear a ship in half? The damage I'm seeing is inconceivable," Kandra Rene said.

"Either the Boxans have some new technology, or there's a new alien species taking part in our war," Mar Arden said.

"This will change things for us. If they can protect entire star systems with a massive barrier, I'm not sure what we can do about that," Kandra Rene said.

"That's the problem we'll need to overcome. Also, things aren't as bleak as they seem. We're inside the barrier. Our mission here is still the same. How we go about achieving our objectives will change, but our goals haven't. The Boxans are keen to protect the Humans for some reason. I'd like to know why that is, wouldn't you?" Mar Arden asked.

"I see your point. Do you think Garm Antis survived?" Kandra Rene asked.

A flash of irritation flicked through his mind at the question.

"If anyone could survive, it would be him. He didn't achieve his position by taking foolish risks, and his flagship was among the rearmost lines."

"Won't the remaining fleet try to get through the barrier?"

"I'm sure they will."

"Should we work to try to open the barrier from the inside rather than travel to Earth?" Kandra Rene asked.

"No, for a couple of reasons. One, the ship is severely damaged. I doubt any of the weapons systems are working, and without main power those systems will never work. Two, if we stay out here, trying to bring down the barrier, we run the risk of drawing attention to ourselves, and without any combat capability to speak of, that would be disastrous for all of us. Third, the Boxans want to keep us from the Humans. We know that some of them are able to resist compulsion, and some of them can't. That alone would pique the Boxans' interest, as it does my own, but there must be more than that. We know their own fleet is limited, and yet they sent three Dreadnaught-class starships to defend this system, and you can be sure there will be more Boxans coming to this system. While we were able to take the first Dreadnaught by surprise, there was no such luck with the second two. Standard Boxan protocol would be to send a communications drone back to their command central, so the fight for this star system is only beginning, and we're in the unique position to influence events in our favor," Mar Arden said.

There was a long pause, which Mar Arden expected.

"Understood, we'll continue our sweep and work our way back to you," Kandra Rene said.

The comms channel closed. Kandra Rene would take some

262 | KEN LOZITO

time to consider what he'd told her, and he was confident that she would agree with his conclusions. If not, or if any other bridge officers began to show signs of doing anything other than following his commands, they would meet with an untimely end. He was in command.

Mar Arden glanced down at Hoan Berend's unconscious form. There was bruising on his face where Mar Arden had hit him, but Mar Arden preferred not to kill him. The commander did have his uses and was resourceful, and once Hoan Berend woke up and learned what had happened, he would likely go along with Mar Arden's plans. That is, of course, until he had the opportunity to betray him, but in Mar Arden's mind, Hoan Berend wasn't a real threat. Rather, he was a tool that needed to learn his place.

CHAPTER FORTY-TWO

Astronomers had theorized that when the solar system was formed, the Earth may have had more than one moon. Some astronomers believed that during this violent period billions of years ago, there had been a second and possibly a third moon that had become part of the Earth's orbit while it was still forming. Ed Johnson had never ascribed to one theory or another; it was just one of those interesting things scientists speculated about.

Ed stood outside under the night sky in the foothills of the Rocky Mountains and glanced up at what many were calling the new moon. It was significantly smaller than the old moon, but it was still something to see. He took a sip from his flask, and the warm, sweet taste of Kentucky bourbon whiskey washed down his throat. He'd found a bottle of Blanton's in one of the offices underground in the command center. After what they'd all been through, taking a bit of someone's bourbon was the least of his problems. He'd have Iris send them a case.

He took another sip and raised his flask in a silent salute to Colonel Kyle Matthews, who, along with several hundred Boxans, had managed to do the impossible. The analysts were calling it a near miss. Regardless of what anyone called it, the people of Earth, and perhaps even the planet itself, had been given a reprieve, another chance to survive in this rapidly changing world they'd become part of. They'd lost communication with Prax'pedax, and a memorial service was planned to honor the Boxans who had sacrificed themselves to protect the Earth. When they'd lost communication with Prax'pedax, they'd also lost all communication beyond a certain point in the solar system. The surviving Boxans were just as perplexed about this as the space agencies of Earth, which was at once comforting and a bit alarming.

Ed found himself wondering whether his late friend, Bruce Matherson, had any idea what had been truly coming for them. First, they'd received that strange alien signal during the nineteen-eighties, and then in the year twenty-fifteen they'd intercepted the first images of Pluto from the spaceship New Horizons, proving that intelligent life did exist beyond their solar system.

Ed heard the crunching footsteps of someone crossing the parking lot, but he wasn't alarmed. Iris wouldn't let anything happen to him. General William Sheridan gave him a nod in greeting and leaned on the car next to Ed.

"You going to share that, or is this a private party?" Sheridan said.

Ed passed him his flask.

"Bourbon. I figured you for a scotch kind of man," Sheridan said and passed the flask back to Ed.

"Scotch is overrated," Ed said.

Sheridan sighed and looked up at the night sky. "Quite a view, isn't it?"

"Yes, it is. I'm not sure how long it will take to get used to it," Ed said.

"Might not get the chance. Once the eggheads decide where to put the thing, we'll be going to work on it. That asteroid is full of rich minerals and a bunch of stuff I can't even begin to understand, but the Boxans believe we can build spaceships with it," Sheridan said.

Ed pressed his lips together and nodded. He hadn't known that. "It's a shame about the Endurance," Ed said.

"The crew survived, and that's what was important. After saving all our collective asses, that is. The Endurance was part of the old world. We'll salvage what we can and use it to build something better—something we can use against the Xiiginns," Sheridan said.

"What about Kyle Matthews and the rest of his crew?" Ed asked.

Sheridan snorted, which sounded a bit like the bark of an old bull mastiff he'd once had. "We'll give them medals, of course. They asked for some time to visit their families, and then we'll put them back to work. I'm relying on the president to put everyone else back to work."

"I think with everything that's happened, we'll get the full support of most nations," Ed said.

"One would think that, but I'll never underestimate another nation's willingness to exploit any event to fuel their own agenda, which may not necessarily align with ours."

266 | KEN LOZITO

"Let me guess—our old friends from China, Russia, and India?" Ed said.

"India has already reached out to me through official ECF channels. Russia and China officials are still considering their position," Sheridan said.

"That stance won't work for them for very long. The Boxans have already said they'll only work with nations who are backing the ECF," Ed said.

Sheridan nodded. "One day at a time. I want to focus our resources on building a fleet of ships and defense platforms capable of going toe-to-toe with the best the Xiiginns have to offer. We'll need training and qualified people for the ECF, and the remaining Boxans are willing to help with that. For a little while there I almost thought we'd be fighting the Boxans, but I'm glad I was wrong about that."

"I think we have the crew of the Athena to thank for that," Ed said.

Sheridan arched an eyebrow. "You still believe they're out there?"

"Without a doubt. Gary Hunter told me they started to receive an incoming data burst that got cut off. The headers for the encryption key was from the Athena. I have no evidence to back this up, but I think they had something to do with whatever cut off the Xiiginn fleet," Ed said.

"Then where the hell are they?"

"An excellent question," Ed said and wished he knew the answer to that.

"I've moved Gary Hunter to the ECF. He's a smart one. Thanks for the recommendation," Sheridan said.

"There'll be more coming," Ed said.

Sheridan eyed him for a moment. "About that. How do you fit into the ECF?"

Ed had been expecting this. "I'm still head of Dux Corp, so I can't exactly be reporting to you," he said.

"That's bullshit, and you know it."

Ed laughed. "How about as a consultant? And I'll bring the best and brightest with me to help."

Sheridan shook his head and gave Ed an appraising look. "You already know I'll take what I can get. There's no room here for petty stubbornness, but I do have a question, just between you and me."

"Alright," Ed said.

"Why not come out of the shadows and officially become part of the ECF? My understanding is that most of the charter was put together by Dux Corp anyway," Sheridan said.

Ed handed the general the flask. "It has nothing to do with you. I want the ECF to work. I believe it's our only shot of surviving, but the way things are today, it's better to be a silent partner rather than become absorbed into the fold. Dux Corp and its subsidiaries remaining separate from the ECF is good for you. It will allow us to act in such a way that it won't hurt the ECF in the long run. It has ever been our mission to ensure that humanity survives its inevitable first contact with an alien race."

Sheridan took a sip from the flask. "If I didn't know better, I'd suspect you were trying to get me drunk to soften the rejection."

"That would be a waste of time. In this, your reputation precedes you. I already know you can drink me under the table," Ed replied.

Sheridan regarded him for a moment. "You're a dangerous man, Ed."

"No more than you are," Ed said.

They heard the high-pitched whine of a rotorless chopper coming toward them. Ed glanced at Iris, who was waiting a short distance away. Iris gave him a single nod.

"Looks like my ride is here. I'll be in touch," Ed said. "Oh, and one more thing. Michael Hunsicker is another good man for the ECF. Currently, he's the foremost expert in dealing with the Boxans."

Sheridan waved him off. Ed climbed into the chopper along with Iris. As always, there was a mountain's worth of work to be done. Unfortunately, they had no idea how much of a reprieve from the threat of the Xiiginns they really had.

CHAPTER FORTY-THREE

I t had been a week since the Athena had left the Sol system. They hadn't gone to the Boxan colony yet because Klado-maor's ship was in desperate need of repairs, and the crew of the Athena used the time to get some much-needed rest. Both ships were taking refuge in a lifeless star system. After their initial jump, the gravity tether had begun to fail, which necessitated them changing their plans. Although the intention had been to pick a star system known to the Boxans, they'd discovered that the navigation database on the Athena held coordinates to star systems that were not known to the Boxans, one of which was relatively close. They'd decided to head there and make as many repairs as they could to Kladomaor's ship while getting better acquainted with the new and improved Athena.

Kaylan was on an EVA with Zack and Hicks, along with Vitomir. They were checking the exterior hull, which was made up of a radically more advanced ceramic composite than their previous hull had been, and Kladomaor had told them they could run a more thorough analysis once they reached the colony. There were still parts of the ship she didn't know the function of, but she, along with the rest of the crew, was going through the information left for them by the Drar AI. Their own AI had retained its identity during the change, which Kaylan appreciated. They'd all come to rely on and trust the Athena's AI, and Zack continued to work with it so—as he liked to put it—it would stop scaring the crap out of them.

"You know, with all the things the Drars did to the ship, I can't believe they didn't give us some kind of super weapon," Zack said.

"It might have been helpful," Hicks agreed.

"I don't think that was their intention at all," Kaylan said. "From the AI's perspective, they were tired of war. There's still a lot of information to go through, and there could be something there, but I seriously doubt they gave us a super weapon. It wouldn't solve the problem they were most interested in, regardless."

"What problem is that?" Zack asked.

"They were looking for a way to stop all the fighting. The Drars fought other races and each other. It's still unclear where they all went," Kaylan said.

"They were able to block your ability and alleviate Jonah's condition for however brief a period of time. That alone is valuable," Zack said.

Hicks laughed. "I think Zack is just upset that he can't hide from you anymore."

Kaylan laughed.

"What? Oh, come on, that's not it at all," Zack said in a teasing manner but then became serious again. "I've been thinking about what it will be like when we finally do get to the Boxan colony."

Kaylan nodded. "I see what you mean. Ma'jasalax has hinted that there are different factions within the Boxans and the Mardoxian sect in particular."

"Exactly. Now, I trust Kladomaor, Gaarokk, Ma'jasalax, and the rest of his crew. It's the others we haven't met that concern me," Zack said.

"One thing at a time," Kaylan said.

Kaylan glanced over at the Boxan stealth ship. It was still heavily damaged, but they'd been working to get it stable enough to return to the colony. Kladomaor had sent out a communications drone, alerting the colony of their intention to return. He'd explained to them that if he hadn't done that, they would run the risk of being fired on by his own species. Kaylan was no stranger to taking a cautious approach to things, but the Boxans took precautions to a whole new level. At first it had seemed like overkill to her, but given what the Boxans had faced and the loss of their own home world, could she really blame them for the steps they'd taken to safeguard the Boxans who were left? And would the people of Earth have to do something similar at some point? She hoped not, but she couldn't be sure circumstances wouldn't require such actions.

They headed back to the airlock, and Kaylan took one last look around. Views of the entire galaxy, such as this one, were almost becoming routine for her, and she wanted to make sure that she stopped every now and then and appreciated the beautiful and mysterious majesty that was their universe.

AFTERWORD

THANK YOU FOR READING INFINITY'S EDGE.

If you loved this book, please consider leaving a review. Comments and reviews allow readers to discover authors, so if you want others to enjoy *Infinity's Edge* as you have, please leave a short note.

If you would like to be notified when my next book is released please visit kenlozito.com and sign up to get a heads up.

The series continues with the 5th book.
Rising Force

ABOUT THE AUTHOR

Ken Lozito is the author of multiple science fiction and fantasy series. I've been reading both science fiction and fantasy for a long time. Books were my way to escape everyday life of a teenager to my current ripe old(?) age. What started out as a love of stories has turned into a full-blown passion for writing them. My ultimate intent for writing stories is to provide fun escapism for readers. I write stories that I would like to read and I hope you enjoy them as well.

If you have questions or comments about any of my works I would love to hear from you, even if its only to drop by to say hello at KenLozito.com

Thanks again for reading *Infinity's Edge.*

Don't be shy about emails, I love getting them, and try to respond to everyone.

Connect with me at the following:
www.kenlozito.com
ken@kenlozito.com

ALSO BY KEN LOZITO

ECHOES OF A GLORIED PAST

AMIDST THE RISING SHADOWS

HEIR OF SHANDARA

BROKEN CROWN SERIES

Haven of Shadows

IF YOU WOULD LIKE TO BE NOTIFIED WHEN MY NEXT BOOK IS
RELEASED VISIT KENLOZITO.COM